Tom Sawyer, Detective

Tom Sawyer, Detective

As told by Huck Finn

Mark Twain

ET REMOTISSIMA PROPE

Hesperus Classics

Hesperus Classics
Published by Hesperus Press Limited
4 Rickett Street, London SW6 1RU
www.hesperuspress.com

First published in 1896
First published by Hesperus Press Limited, 2004

Designed and typeset by Fraser Muggeridge
Printed in Italy by Graphic Studio Srl

ISBN: 1-84391-081-0

CONTENTS

Tom Sawyer, Detective

CHAPTER ONE

An Invitation for Tom and Huck

Well, it was the next spring after me and Tom Sawyer set our old nigger Jim free, the time he was chained up for a runaway slave down there on Tom's Uncle Silas' farm in Arkansaw.[1] The frost was working out of the ground, and out of the air too, and it was getting closer and closer onto barefoot time every day; and next it would be marble time, and next mum bletypeg[2], and next tops and hoops, and next kites, and then right away it would be summer and going in a-swimming. It just makes a boy homesick to look ahead like that and see how far off summer is. Yes, and it sets him to sighing and saddening around, and there's something the matter with him, he don't know what. But anyway, he gets out by himself and mopes and thinks; and mostly he hunts for a lonesome place high up on the hill in the edge of the woods, and sets there and looks away off on the big Mississippi down there a-reaching miles and miles around the points where the timber looks smoky and dim it's so far off and still, and everything's so solemn it seems like everybody you've loved is dead and gone, and you 'most wish you was dead and gone too, and done with it all.

Don't you know what that is? It's spring fever. That is what the name of it is. And when you've got it, you want – oh, you don't quite know what it is you *do* want, but it just fairly makes your heart ache, you want it so! It seems to you that mainly what you want is to get away; get away from the same old tedious things you're so used to seeing and so tired of, and see something new. That is the idea; you want to go and be a wanderer; you want to go wandering far away to strange countries where everything is mysterious and wonderful and romantic. And if you can't do that, you'll put up with considerable less; you'll go anywhere you *can* go, just so as to get away, and be thankful of the chance, too.

Well, me and Tom Sawyer had the spring fever, and had it bad, too; but it warn't any use to think about Tom trying to get away, because, as he said, his Aunt Polly wouldn't let him quit school and go traipsing off somers wasting time; so we was pretty blue. We was setting on the front steps one day about sundown talking this way, when out comes his Aunt Polly with a letter in her hand and says –

'Tom, I reckon you've got to pack up and go down to Arkansaw – your Aunt Sally wants you.'

I 'most jumped out of my skin for joy. I reckoned Tom would fly at his aunt and hug her head off; but if you believe me he set there like a rock, and never said a word. It made me fit to cry to see him act so foolish, with such a noble chance as this opening up. Why, we might lose it if he didn't speak up and show he was thankful and grateful. But he set there and studied and studied till I was that distressed I didn't know what to do; then he says, very ca'm, and I could a shot him for it:

'Well,' he says, 'I'm right down sorry, Aunt Polly, but I reckon I got to be excused – for the present.'

His Aunt Polly was knocked so stupid and so mad at the cold impudence of it that she couldn't say a word for as much as a half a minute, and this gave me a chance to nudge Tom and whisper:

'Ain't you got any sense? Sp'iling such a noble chance as this and throwing it away?'

But he warn't disturbed. He mumbled back:

'Huck Finn, do you want me to let her *see* how bad I want to go? Why, she'd begin to doubt, right away, and imagine a lot of sicknesses and dangers and objections, and first you know she'd take it all back. You lemme alone; I reckon I know how to work her.'

Now I never would a thought of that. But he was right. Tom Sawyer was always right – the levelest head I ever see, and always *at* himself and ready for anything you might spring on him. By this time his Aunt Polly was all straight again, and she let fly. She says:

'You'll be excused! *You* will! Well, I never heard the like of it in all my days! The idea of you talking like that to *me*! Now take yourself off and pack your traps; and if I hear another word out of you about what you'll be excused from and what you won't, I lay *I'll* excuse you – with a hickory!'

She hit his head a thump with her thimble as we dodged by, and he let on to be whimpering as we struck for the stairs. Up in his room he hugged me; he was so out of his head for gladness because he was going traveling. And he says:

'Before we get away she'll wish she hadn't let me go, but she won't know any way to get around it now. After what she's said, her pride won't let her take it back.'

Tom was packed in ten minutes, all except what his aunt and Mary would finish up for him; then we waited ten more for her to get cooled down and sweet and gentle again; for Tom said it took her ten minutes to unruffle in times when half of her feathers was up, but twenty when they was all up, and this was one of the times when they was all up. Then we went down, being in a sweat to know what the letter said.

She was setting there in a brown study, with it laying in her lap. We set down, and she says:

'They're in considerable trouble down there, and they think you and Huck'll be a kind of diversion for them – "comfort", they say. Much of that they'll get out of you and Huck Finn, I reckon. There's a neighbor named Brace Dunlap that's been wanting to marry their Benny for three months, and at last they told him pine-blank[3] and once for all, he *couldn't*; so he has soured on them, and they're worried about it. I reckon he's somebody they think they better be on the good side of, for they've tried to please him by hiring his no-account brother to help on the farm when they can't hardly afford it, and don't want him around anyhow. Who are the Dunlaps?'

'They live about a mile from Uncle Silas' place, Aunt Polly – all the farmers live about a mile apart down there – and Brace Dunlap is a long sight richer than any of the others, and owns a whole grist of niggers. He's a widower, thirty-six years old, without any children, and is proud of his money and over-bearing, and everybody is a little afraid of him. I judge he thought he could have any girl he wanted, just for the asking, and it must have set him back a good deal when he found he couldn't get Benny. Why, Benny's only half as old as he is, and just as sweet and lovely as – well, you've seen her. Poor old Uncle Silas – why, it's pitiful, him trying to curry favor that way – so hard pushed and poor, and yet hiring that useless Jubiter Dunlap to please his ornery brother.'

'What a name – Jubiter! Where'd he get it?'

'It's only just a nickname. I reckon they've forgot his real name long before this. He's twenty-seven, now, and has had it ever since the first time he ever went in swimming. The school teacher seen a round brown mole the size of a dime on his left leg above his knee, and four little bits of moles around it, when he was naked, and he said it minded him of Jubiter and his moons; and the children thought it was funny, and so they got to calling him Jubiter, and he's Jubiter yet. He's tall, and lazy, and sly, and sneaky, and ruther cowardly, too, but kind of good-natured, and wears long brown hair and no beard, and hasn't got a cent, and Brace boards him for nothing, and gives him his old clothes to wear, and despises him. Jubiter is a twin.'

'What's t'other twin like?'

'Just exactly like Jubiter – so they say; used to was, anyway, but he hain't been seen for seven years. He got to robbing when he was nineteen or twenty, and they jailed him; but he broke jail and got away – up north here, somers. They used to hear about him robbing and burglaring now and then, but that was years ago. He's dead, now. At least that's what they say. They don't hear about him any more.'

'What was his name?'

'Jake.'

There wasn't anything more said for a considerable while; the old lady was thinking. At last she says:

'The thing that is mostly worrying your Aunt Sally is the tempers that that man Jubiter gets your uncle into.'

Tom was astonished, and so was I. Tom says:

'Tempers? Uncle Silas? Land, you must be joking! I didn't know he *had* any temper.'

'Works him up into perfect rages, your Aunt Sally says; says he acts as if he would really hit the man, sometimes.'

'Aunt Polly, it beats anything I ever heard of. Why, he's just as gentle as mush.'

'Well, she's worried, anyway. Says your Uncle Silas is like a changed man, on account of all this quarreling. And the neighbors talk about it, and lay all the blame on your uncle, of course, because he's a preacher and hain't got any business to quarrel. Your Aunt Sally says he hates to go into the pulpit he's so ashamed; and the people have begun to cool toward him, and he ain't as popular now as he used to was.'

'Well, ain't it strange? Why, Aunt Polly, he was always so good and kind and moony and absent-minded and chuckle-headed and lovable – why, he was just an angel! What *can* be the matter of him, do you reckon?'

CHAPTER TWO

Jake Dunlap

We had powerful good luck; because we got a chance in a stern-wheeler from away north which was bound for one of them bayous[4] or one-horse rivers away down Louisiana way, and so we could go all the way down the Upper Mississippi and all the way down the Lower Mississippi to that farm in Arkansaw without having to change steamboats at St Louis; not so very much short of a thousand miles at one pull.

A pretty lonesome boat; there warn't but few passengers, and all old folks, that set around, wide apart, dozing, and was very quiet. We was four days getting out of the 'upper river', because we got aground so much. But it warn't dull – couldn't be for boys that was traveling, of course.

From the very start me and Tom allowed that there was somebody sick in the stateroom next to ourn, because the meals was always toted in there by the waiters. By and by we asked about it – Tom did – and the waiter said it was a man, but he didn't look sick.

'Well, but *ain't* he sick?'

'I don't know; maybe he is, but 'pears to me he's just letting on.'

'What makes you think that?'

'Because if he was sick he would pull his clothes off *some* time or other – don't you reckon he would? Well, this one don't. At least he don't ever pull off his boots, anyway.'

'The mischief he don't! Not even when he goes to bed?'

'No.'

It was always nuts for Tom Sawyer – a mystery was. If you'd

lay out a mystery and a pie before me and him, you wouldn't have to say take your choice; it was a thing that would regulate itself. Because in my nature I have always run to pie, whilst in his nature he has always run to mystery. People are made different. And it is the best way. Tom says to the waiter:

'What's the man's name?'

'Phillips.'

'Where'd he come aboard?'

'I think he got aboard at Elexandria, up on the Iowa line.'

'What do you reckon he's a-playing?'

'I hain't any notion – I never thought of it.'

I says to myself, here's another one that runs to pie.

'Anything peculiar about him? – the way he acts or talks?'

'No – nothing, except he seems so scary, and keeps his doors locked night and day both, and when you knock he won't let you in till he opens the door a crack and sees who it is.'

'By jimminy, it's int'resting! I'd like to get a look at him. Say – the next time you're going in there, don't you reckon you could spread the door and –'

'No, indeedy! He's always behind it. He would block that game.'

Tom studied over it, and then he says:

'Looky-here. You lend me your apern and let me take him his breakfast in the morning. I'll give you a quarter.'

The boy was plenty willing enough, if the head steward wouldn't mind. Tom says that's all right, he reckoned he could fix it with the head steward; and he done it. He fixed it so as we could both go in with aperns on and toting vittles.

He didn't sleep much, he was in such a sweat to get in there and find out the mystery about Phillips; and moreover he done a lot of guessing about it all night, which warn't no use, for if you are going to find out the facts of a thing, what's the sense in guessing out what ain't the facts and wasting ammunition? I didn't lose no sleep. I wouldn't give a dern to know what's the matter of Phillips, I says to myself.

Well, in the morning we put on the aperns and got a couple of trays of truck, and Tom he knocked on the door. The man opened it a crack, and then he let us in and shut it quick. By Jackson, when we got a sight of him, we 'most dropped the trays! and Tom says:

'Why, Jubiter Dunlap, where'd *you* come from?'

Well, the man was astonished, of course; and first off he looked like he didn't know whether to be scared, or glad, or both, or which, but finally he settled down to being glad; and then his color come back, though at first his face had turned pretty white. So we got to talking together while he et his breakfast. And he says:

'But I ain't Jubiter Dunlap. I'd just as soon tell you who I am, though, if you'll swear to keep mum, for I ain't no Phillips, either.'

Tom says:

'We'll keep mum, but there ain't any need to tell who you are if you ain't Jubiter Dunlap.'

'Why?'

'Because if you ain't him you're t'other twin, Jake. You're the spit'n image of Jubiter.'

'Well, I am Jake. But looky-here, how do you come to know us Dunlaps?'

Tom told about the adventures we'd had down there at his Uncle Silas' last summer, and when he see that there warn't anything about his folks – or him either, for that matter – that we didn't know, he opened out and talked perfectly free and candid. He never made any bones about his own case; said

11

he'd been a hard lot, was a hard lot yet, and reckoned he'd *be* a hard lot plumb to the end. He said of course it was a dangerous life, and –

He give a kind of gasp, and set his head like a person that's listening. We didn't say anything, and so it was very still for a second or so, and there warn't no sounds but the screaking of the woodwork and the chug- chugging of the machinery down below.

Then we got him comfortable again, telling him about his people, and how Brace's wife had been dead three years, and Brace wanted to marry Benny and she shook him, and Jubiter was working for Uncle Silas, and him and Uncle Silas quarreling all the time – and then he let go and laughed.

'Land!' he says, 'it's like old times to hear all this tittle-tattle, and does me good. It's been seven years and more since I heard any. How do they talk about me these days?'

'Who?'

'The farmers – and the family.'

'Why, they don't talk about you at all – at least only just a mention, once in a long time.'

'The nation!' he says, surprised; 'why is that?'

'Because they think you are dead long ago.'

'No! Are you speaking true? – honor bright, now.' He jumped up, excited.

'Honor bright. There ain't anybody thinks you are alive.'

'Then I'm saved, I'm saved, sure! I'll go home. They'll hide me and save my life. You keep mum. Swear you'll keep mum – swear you'll never, never tell on me. Oh, boys, be good to a poor devil that's being hunted day and night, and dasn't show his face! I've never done you any harm; I'll never do you any, as God is in the heavens; swear you'll be good to me and help me save my life.'

We'd a swore it if he'd been a dog; and so we done it. Well, he couldn't love us enough for it or be grateful enough, poor cuss; it was all he could do to keep from hugging us.

We talked along, and he got out a little handbag and begun to open it, and told us to turn our backs. We done it, and when he told us to turn again he was perfectly different to what he was before. He had on blue goggles and the naturalest-looking long brown whiskers and mustashes you ever see. His own mother wouldn't a knowed him. He asked us if he looked like his brother Jubiter, now.

'No,' Tom said; 'there ain't anything left that's like him except the long hair.'

'All right, I'll get that cropped close to my head before I get there; then him and Brace will keep my secret, and I'll live with them as being a stranger, and the neighbors won't ever guess me out. What do you think?'

Tom he studied awhile, then he says:

'Well, of course me and Huck are going to keep mum there, but if you don't keep mum yourself there's going to be a little bit of a risk – it ain't much, maybe, but it's a little. I mean, if you talk, won't people notice that your voice is just like Jubiter's; and mightn't it make them think of the twin they reckoned was dead, but maybe after all was hid all this time under another name?'

'By George,' he says, 'you're a sharp one! You're perfectly right. I've got to play deef and dumb when there's a neighbor around. If I'd a struck for home and forgot that little detail – However, I wasn't striking for home. I was breaking for any place where I could get away from these fellows that are after me; then I was going to put on this disguise and get some different clothes, and –'

He jumped for the outside door and laid his ear against it

and listened, pale and kind of panting. Presently he whispers:

'Sounded like cocking a gun! Lord, what a life to lead!'

Then he sunk down in a chair all limp and sick like, and wiped the sweat off of his face.

CHAPTER THREE

A Diamond Robbery

From that time out, we was with him 'most all the time, and one or t'other of us slept in his upper berth. He said he had been so lonesome, and it was such a comfort to him to have company, and somebody to talk to in his troubles. We was in a sweat to find out what his secret was, but Tom said the best way was not to seem anxious, then likely he would drop into it himself in one of his talks, but if we got to asking questions he would get suspicious and shet up his shell. It turned out just so. It warn't no trouble to see that he *wanted* to talk about it, but always along at first he would scare away from it when he got on the very edge of it, and go to talking about something else. The way it come about was this: He got to asking us, kind of indifferent like, about the passengers down on deck. We told him about them. But he warn't satisfied; we warn't particular enough. He told us to describe them better. Tom done it. At last, when Tom was describing one of the roughest and raggedest ones, he gave a shiver and a gasp and says:

'Oh, lordy, that's one of them! They're aboard sure – I just knowed it. I sort of hoped I had got away, but I never believed it. Go on.'

Presently when Tom was describing another mangy, rough deck passenger, he give that shiver again and says:

'That's him! – that's the other one. If it would only come a good black stormy night and I could get ashore. You see, they've got spies on me. They've got a right to come up and buy drinks at the bar yonder forrard, and they take that chance to bribe somebody to keep watch on me – porter or boots or somebody. If I was to slip ashore without anybody seeing me, they would know it inside of an hour.'

So then he got to wandering along, and pretty soon, sure enough, he was telling! He was poking along through his ups and downs, and when he come to that place he went right along. He says:

'It was a confidence game. We played it on a julery-shop in St Louis. What we was after was a couple of noble big di'monds as big as hazelnuts, which everybody was running to see. We was dressed up fine, and we played it on them in broad daylight. We ordered the di'monds sent to the hotel for us to see if we wanted to buy, and when we was examining them we had paste counterfeits all ready, and *them* was the things that went back to the shop when we said the water wasn't quite fine enough for twelve thousand dollars.'

'Twelve thousand dollars!' Tom says. 'Was they really worth all that money, do you reckon?'

'Every cent of it.'

'And you fellows got away with them?'

'As easy as nothing. I don't reckon the julery people know they've been robbed yet. But it wouldn't be good sense to stay around St Louis, of course, so we considered where we'd go. One was for going one way, one another, so we throwed up, heads or tails, and the Upper Mississippi won. We done up the di'monds in a paper and put our names on it and put it in the keep of the hotel clerk, and told him not to ever let either of us have it again without the others was on hand to see it done; then we went down town, each by his own self – because I reckon maybe we all had the same notion. I don't know for certain, but I reckon maybe we had.'

'What notion?' Tom says.

'To rob the others.'

'What – one take everything, after all of you had helped to get it?'

'Cert'nly.'

It disgusted Tom Sawyer, and he said it was the orneriest, low-downest thing he ever heard of. But Jake Dunlap said it warn't unusual in the profession. Said when a person was in that line of business he'd got to look out for his own intrust, there warn't nobody else going to do it for him. And then he went on. He says:

'You see, the trouble was, you couldn't divide up two di'monds amongst three. If there'd been three – but never mind about that, there warn't three. I loafed along the back-streets studying and studying. And I says to myself, I'll hog them di'monds the first chance I get, and I'll have a disguise all ready, and I'll give the boys the slip, and when I'm safe away I'll put it on, and then let them find me if they can. So I got the false whiskers and the goggles and this countrified suit of clothes, and fetched them along back in a handbag; and when I was passing a shop where they sell all sorts of things, I got a glimpse of one of my pals through the window. It was Bud Dixon. I was glad, you bet. I says to myself, I'll see what he buys. So I kept shady, and watched. Now what do you reckon it was he bought?'

'Whiskers?' said I.

'No.'

'Goggles?'

'No.'

'Oh, keep still, Huck Finn, can't you, you're only just hendering all you can. What *was* it he bought, Jake?'

'You'd never guess in the world. It was only just a screwdriver – just a wee little bit of a screwdriver.'

'Well, I declare! What did he want with that?'

'That's what *I* thought. It was curious. It clean stumped me. I says to myself, what can he want with that thing? Well, when he come out I stood back out of sight, and then tracked him to a second-hand slop-shop and see him buy a red flannel shirt and some old ragged clothes – just the ones he's got on now, as you've described. Then I went down to the wharf and hid my things aboard the up-river boat that we had picked out, and then started back and had another streak of luck. I seen our other pal lay in *his* stock of old rusty second-handers. We got the di'monds and went aboard the boat.

'But now we was up a stump, for we couldn't go to bed. We had to set up and watch one another. Pity, that was; pity to put that kind of a strain on us, because there was bad blood between us from a couple of weeks back, and we was only friends in the way of business. Bad anyway, seeing there was only two di'monds betwixt three men. First we had supper, and then tramped up and down the deck together smoking till 'most midnight; then we went and set down in my stateroom and locked the doors and looked in the piece of paper to see if the di'monds was all right, then laid it on the lower berth right in full sight; and there we set, and set, and by and by it got to be dreadful hard to keep awake. At last Bud Dixon he dropped off. As soon as he was snoring a good regular gait that was likely to last, and had his chin on his breast and looked permanent, Hal Clayton nodded towards the di'monds and then towards the outside door, and I understood. I reached and got the paper, and then we stood up and waited perfectly still; Bud never stirred; I turned the key of the outside door very soft and slow, then turned the knob the same way, and we went tiptoeing out onto the guard, and shut the door very soft and gentle.

'There warn't nobody stirring anywhere, and the boat was

slipping along, swift and steady, through the big water in the smoky moonlight. We never said a word, but went straight up onto the hurricane-deck and plumb back aft, and set down on the end of the skylight. Both of us knowed what that meant, without having to explain to one another. Bud Dixon would wake up and miss the swag, and would come straight for us, for he ain't afeard of anything or anybody, that man ain't. He would come, and we would heave him overboard, or get killed trying. It made me shiver, because I ain't as brave as some people, but if I showed the white feather – well, I knowed better than do that. I kind of hoped the boat would land somers, and we could skip ashore and not have to run the risk of this row, I was so scared of Bud Dixon, but she was an upper-river tub and there warn't no real chance of that.

'Well, the time strung along and along, and that fellow never come! Why, it strung along till dawn begun to break, and still he never come. "Thunder," I says, "what do you make out of this? – ain't it suspicious?" "Land!" Hal says, "do you reckon he's playing us? – open the paper!" I done it, and by gracious there warn't anything in it but a couple of little pieces of loaf-sugar! *That's* the reason he could set there and snooze all night so comfortable. Smart? Well, I reckon! He had had them two papers all fixed and ready, and he had put one of them in place of t'other right under our noses.

'We felt pretty cheap. But the thing to do, straight off, was to make a plan; and we done it. We would do up the paper again, just as it was, and slip in, very elaborate and soft, and lay it on the bunk again, and let on *we* didn't know about any trick, and hadn't any idea he was a-laughing at us behind them bogus snores of his'n; and we would stick by him, and the first night we was ashore we would get him drunk and search him, and get the di'monds; and *do* for him, too, if it warn't too risky.

If we got the swag, we'd *got* to do for him, or he would hunt us down and do for us, sure. But I didn't have no real hope. I knowed we could get him drunk – he was always ready for that – but what's the good of it? You might search him a year and never find –

'Well, right there I catched my breath and broke off my thought! For an idea went ripping through my head that tore my brains to rags – and land, but I felt gay and good! You see, I had had my boots off, to unswell my feet, and just then I took up one of them to put it on, and I catched a glimpse of the heel bottom, and it just took my breath away. You remember about that puzzlesome little screwdriver?'

'You bet I do,' says Tom, all excited.

'Well, when I catched that glimpse of that boot heel, the idea that went smashing through my head was, *I* know where he's hid the di'monds! You look at this boot heel, now. See, it's bottomed with a steel plate, and the plate is fastened on with little screws. Now there wasn't a screw about that feller anywhere but in his boot heels; so, if he needed a screwdriver, I reckoned I knowed why.'

'Huck, ain't it bully!' says Tom.

'Well, I got my boots on, and we went down and slipped in and laid the paper of sugar on the berth, and sat down soft and sheepish and went to listening to Bud Dixon snore. Hal Clayton dropped off pretty soon, but I didn't; I wasn't ever so wide awake in my life. I was spying out from under the shade of my hat brim, searching the floor for leather. It took me a long time, and I begun to think maybe my guess was wrong, but at last I struck it. It laid over by the bulkhead, and was nearly the color of the carpet. It was a little round plug about as thick as the end of your little finger, and I says to myself there's a di'mond in the nest you've come from. Before long

I spied out the plug's mate.

'Think of the smartness and coolness of that blatherskite! He put up that scheme on us and reasoned out what we would do, and we went ahead and done it perfectly exact, like a couple of pudd'n-heads. He set there and took his own time to unscrew his heelplates and cut out his plugs and stick in the di'monds and screw on his plates again. He allowed we would steal the bogus swag and wait all night for him to come up and get drownded, and by George it's just what we done! I think it was powerful smart.'

'You bet your life it was!' says Tom, just full of admiration.

CHAPTER FOUR

The Three Sleepers

'Well, all day we went through the humbug of watching one another, and it was pretty sickly business for two of us and hard to act out, I can tell you. About night we landed at one of them little Missouri towns high up toward Iowa, and had supper at the tavern, and got a room upstairs with a cot and a double bed in it, but I dumped my bag under a deal table in the dark hall while we was moving along it to bed, single file, me last, and the landlord in the lead with a tallow candle. We had up a lot of whisky, and went to playing high-low-jack for dimes, and as soon as the whisky begun to take hold of Bud we stopped drinking, but we didn't let him stop. We loaded him till he fell out of his chair and laid there snoring.

'We was ready for business now. I said we better pull our boots off, and his'n too, and not make any noise, then we could pull him and haul him around and ransack him without any trouble. So we done it. I set my boots and Bud's side by side, where they'd be handy. Then we stripped him and searched his seams and his pockets and his socks and the inside of his boots, and everything, and searched his bundle. Never found any di'monds. We found the screwdriver, and Hal says, "What do you reckon he wanted with that?" I said I didn't know; but when he wasn't looking I hooked it. At last Hal he looked beat and discouraged, and said we'd got to give it up. That was what I was waiting for. I says:

' "There's one place we hain't searched."

' "What place is that?" he says.

' "His stomach."

' "By gracious, I never thought of that! *Now* we're on the homestretch, to a dead moral certainty. How'll we manage?"

' "Well," I says, "just stay by him till I turn out and hunt up a drug store, and I reckon I'll fetch something that'll make them di'monds tired of the company they're keeping."

'He said that's the ticket, and with him looking straight at me I slid myself into Bud's boots instead of my own, and he never noticed. They was just a shade large for me, but that was considerable better than being too small. I got my bag as I went a-groping through the hall, and in about a minute I was out the back way and stretching up the river road at a five-mile gait.

'And not feeling so very bad, neither – walking on di'monds don't have no such effect. When I had gone fifteen minutes I says to myself, there's more'n a mile behind me, and everything quiet. Another five minutes and I says there's considerable more land behind me now, and there's a man back there that's begun to wonder what's the trouble. Another five and I says to myself he's getting real uneasy – he's walking the floor now. Another five, and I says to myself, there's two mile and a half behind me, and he's *awful* uneasy – beginning to cuss, I reckon. Pretty soon I says to myself, forty minutes gone – he *knows* there's something up! Fifty minutes – the truth's a-busting on him now! He is reckoning I found the di'monds whilst we was searching, and shoved them in my pocket and never let on – yes, and he's starting out to hunt for me. He'll hunt for new tracks in the dust, and they'll as likely send him down the river as up.

'Just then I see a man coming down on a mule, and before I thought I jumped into the bush. It was stupid! When he got abreast he stopped and waited a little for me to come out; then he rode on again. But I didn't feel gay any more. I says to myself I've botched my chances by that; I surely have, if he meets up with Hal Clayton.

'Well, about three in the morning I fetched Elexandria and see this stern-wheeler laying there, and was very glad, because I felt perfectly safe, now, you know. It was just daybreak. I went aboard and got this state-room and put on these clothes and went up in the pilot-house – to watch, though I didn't reckon there was any need of it. I set there and played with my di'monds and waited and waited for the boat to start, but she didn't. You see, they was mending her machinery, but I didn't know anything about it, not being very much used to steamboats.

'Well, to cut the tale short, we never left there till plumb noon; and long before that I was hid in this state-room; for before breakfast I see a man coming, away off, that had a gait like Hal Clayton's, and it made me just sick. I says to myself, if he finds out I'm aboard this boat, he's got me like a rat in a trap. All he's got to do is to have me watched, and wait – wait till I slip ashore, thinking he is a thousand miles away, then slip after me and dog me to a good place and make me give up the di'monds, and then he'll – oh, I know what he'll do! Ain't it awful – awful! And now to think the *other* one's aboard, too! Oh, ain't it hard luck, boys – ain't it hard! But you'll help save me, *won't* you? – oh, boys, be good to a poor devil that's being hunted to death, and save me – I'll worship the very ground you walk on!'

We turned in and soothed him down and told him we would plan for him and help him, and he needn't be so afeard; and so by and by he got to feeling kind of comfortable again, and unscrewed his heelplates and held up his di'monds this way and that, admiring them and loving them; and when the light struck into them they *was* beautiful, sure; why, they seemed to kind of bust, and snap fire out all around. But all the same I judged he was a fool. If I had been him I would a handed the di'monds to them pals and got them to go ashore and leave me alone. But he was made different. He said it was a whole fortune and he couldn't bear the idea.

Twice we stopped to fix the machinery and laid a good while, once in the night; but it wasn't dark enough, and he was afeard to skip. But the third time we had to fix it there was a better chance. We laid up at a country woodyard about forty mile above Uncle Silas' place, a little after one at night, and it was thickening up and going to storm. So Jake he laid for a chance to slide. We begun to take in wood. Pretty soon the rain come a-drenching down, and the wind blowed hard. Of course every boat-hand fixed a gunny sack and put it on like a bonnet, the way they do when they are toting wood, and we got one for Jake, and he slipped down aft with his handbag and come tramping forrard just like the rest, and walked ashore with them, and when we see him pass out of the light of the torch-basket and get swallowed up in the dark, we got our breath again and just felt grateful and splendid. But it wasn't for long. Somebody told, I reckon; for in about eight or ten minutes them two pals come tearing forrard as tight as they could jump and darted ashore and was gone. We waited plumb till dawn for them to come back, and kept hoping they would, but they never did. We was awful sorry and low-spirited. All the hope we had was that Jake had got such a start that they couldn't get on his track, and he would get to his brother's and hide there and be safe.

He was going to take the river road, and told us to find out if Brace and Jubiter was to home and no strangers there, and then slip out about sundown and tell him. Said he would wait for us in a little bunch of sycamores right back of Tom's Uncle

Silas' tobacker-field on the river road, a lonesome place.

We set and talked a long time about his chances, and Tom said he was all right if the pals struck up the river instead of down, but it wasn't likely, because maybe they knowed where he was from; more likely they would go right, and dog him all day, him not suspecting, and kill him when it come dark, and take the boots. So we was pretty sorrowful.

CHAPTER FIVE

A Tragedy in the Woods

We didn't get done tinkering the machinery till away late in the afternoon, and so it was so close to sundown when we got home that we never stopped on our road, but made a break for the sycamores as tight as we could go, to tell Jake what the delay was, and have him wait till we could go to Brace's and find out how things was there. It was getting pretty dim by the time we turned the corner of the woods, sweating and panting with that long run, and see the sycamores thirty yards ahead of us; and just then we see a couple of men run into the bunch and heard two or three terrible screams for help. 'Poor Jake is killed, sure,' we says. We was scared through and through, and broke for the tobacker-field and hid there, trembling so our clothes would hardly stay on; and just as we skipped in there, a couple of men went tearing by, and into the bunch they went, and in a second out jumps four men and took out up the road as tight as they could go, two chasing two.

We laid down, kind of weak and sick, and listened for more sounds, but didn't hear none for a good while but just our hearts. We was thinking of that awful thing laying yonder in the sycamores, and it seemed like being that close to a ghost, and it give me the cold shudders. The moon come a-swelling up out of the ground, now, powerful big and round and bright, behind a comb of trees, like a face looking through prison bars, and the black shadders and white places begun to creep around, and it was miserable quiet and still and night-breezy and graveyardy and scary.

All of a sudden Tom whispers:

'Look! – what's that?'

'Don't!' I says. 'Don't take a person by surprise that way. I'm 'most ready to die, anyway, without you doing that.'

'Look, I tell you. It's something coming out of the sycamores.'

'Don't, Tom!'

'It's terrible tall!'

'Oh, lordy-lordy! let's –'

'Keep still – it's a-coming this way.'

He was so excited he could hardly get breath enough to whisper. I had to look. I couldn't help it. So now we was both on our knees with our chins on a fence rail and gazing – yes, and gasping too. It was coming down the road – coming in the shadder of the trees, and you couldn't see it good; not till it was pretty close to us; then it stepped into a bright splotch of moonlight and we sunk right down in our tracks – it was Jake Dunlap's ghost! That was what we said to ourselves.

We couldn't stir for a minute or two; then it was gone. We talked about it in low voices. Tom says:

'They're mostly dim and smoky, or like they're made out of fog, but this one wasn't.'

'No,' I says; 'I seen the goggles and the whiskers perfectly plain.'

'Yes, and the very colors in them loud countrified Sunday clothes – plaid breeches, green and black –'

'Cotton velvet westcot, fire-red and yaller squares –'

'Leather straps to the bottoms of the breeches' legs and one of them hanging unbottoned –'

'Yes, and that hat –'

'What a hat for a ghost to wear!'

You see it was the first season anybody wore that kind – a

black stiff-brim stovepipe, very high, and not smooth, with a round top – just like a sugar-loaf.

'Did you notice if its hair was the same, Huck?'

'No – seems to me I did, then again it seems to me I didn't.'

'I didn't either; but it had its bag along, I noticed that.'

'So did I. How can there be a ghost-bag, Tom?'

'Sho! I wouldn't be as ignorant as that if I was you, Huck Finn. Whatever a ghost has, turns to ghost-stuff. They've got to have their things, like anybody else. You see, yourself, that its clothes was turned to ghost-stuff. Well, then, what's to hender its bag from turning, too? Of course it done it.'

That was reasonable. I couldn't find no fault with it. Bill Withers and his brother Jack come along by, talking, and Jack says:

'What do you reckon he was toting?'

'I dunno; but it was pretty heavy.'

'Yes, all he could lug. Nigger stealing corn from old Parson Silas, I judged.'

'So did I. And so I allowed I wouldn't let on to see him.'

'That's me, too.'

Then they both laughed, and went on out of hearing. It showed how unpopular old Uncle Silas had got to be now. They wouldn't a let a nigger steal anybody else's corn and never done anything to him.

We heard some more voices mumbling along towards us and getting louder, and sometimes a cackle of a laugh. It was Lem Beebe and Jim Lane.

Jim Lane says: 'Who? – Jubiter Dunlap?'

'Yes.'

'Oh, I don't know. I reckon so. I seen him spading up some ground along about an hour ago, just before sundown – him and the parson. Said he guessed he wouldn't go tonight, but we could have his dog if we wanted him.'

'Too tired, I reckon.'

'Yes – works so hard!'

'Oh, you bet!'

They cackled at that, and went on by. Tom said we better jump out and tag along after them, because they was going our way and it wouldn't be comfortable to run across the ghost all by ourselves. So we done it, and got home all right.

That night was the 2nd of September – a Saturday. I sha'n't ever forget it. You'll see why, pretty soon.

CHAPTER SIX

Plans to Secure the Diamonds

We tramped along behind Jim and Lem till we come to the back stile where old Jim's cabin was that he was captivated in, the time we set him free, and here come the dogs piling around us to say howdy, and there was the lights of the house, too; so we warn't afeard any more, and was going to climb over, but Tom says:

'Hold on; set down here a minute. By George!'

'What's the matter?' says I.

'Matter enough!' he says. 'Wasn't you expecting we would be the first to tell the family who it is that's been killed yonder in the sycamores, and all about them rapscallions that done it, and about the di'monds they've smouched off of the corpse, and paint it up fine, and have the glory of being the ones that knows a lot more about it than anybody else?'

'Why, of course. It wouldn't be you, Tom Sawyer, if you was to let such a chance go by. I reckon it ain't going to suffer none for lack of paint,' I says, 'when you start in to scollop the facts.'

'Well, now,' he says, perfectly ca'm, 'what would you say if I was to tell you I ain't going to start in at all?'

I was astonished to hear him talk so. I says:

'I'd say it's a lie. You ain't in earnest, Tom Sawyer?'

'You'll soon see. Was the ghost barefooted?'

'No, it wasn't. What of it?'

'You wait – I'll show you what. Did it have its boots on?'

'Yes. I seen them plain.'

'Swear it?'

'Yes, I swear it.'

'So do I. Now do you know what that means?'

'No. What does it mean?'

'Means that them thieves *didn't get the di'monds.*'

'Jimminy! What makes you think that?'

'I don't only think it, I know it. Didn't the breeches and goggles and whiskers and handbag and every blessed thing turn to ghost-stuff? Everything it had on turned, didn't it? It shows that the reason its boots turned too was because it still had them on after it started to go ha'nting around, and if that ain't proof that them blatherskites didn't get the boots, I'd like to know what you'd *call* proof.'

Think of that now. I never see such a head as that boy had. Why, I had eyes and I could see things, but they never meant nothing to me. But Tom Sawyer was different. When Tom Sawyer seen a thing it just got up on its hind legs and *talked* to him – told him everything it knowed. I never see such a head.

'Tom Sawyer,' I says, 'I'll say it again as I've said it a many a time before: I ain't fitten to black your boots. But that's all right – that's neither here nor there. God Almighty made us all, and some He gives eyes that's blind, and some He gives eyes that can see, and I reckon it ain't none of our lookout what He done it for; it's all right, or He'd a fixed it some other way. Go on – I see plenty plain enough, now, that them thieves didn't get way with the di'monds. Why didn't they, do you reckon?'

'Because they got chased away by them other two men before they could pull the boots off of the corpse.'

'That's so! I see it now. But looky here, Tom, why ain't we to go and tell about it?'

'Oh, shucks, Huck Finn, can't you see? Look at it. What's a-going to happen? There's going to be an inquest in the morning. Them two men will tell how they heard the yells and rushed there just in time to not save the stranger. Then the jury'll twaddle and twaddle and twaddle, and finally they'll fetch in a verdict that he got shot or stuck or busted over the head with something, and come to his death by the inspiration of God. And after they've buried him they'll auction off his things for to pay the expenses, and then's *our* chance.'

'How, Tom?'

'Buy the boots for two dollars!'

Well, it 'most took my breath.

'My land! Why, Tom, *we'll* get the di'monds!'

'You bet. Some day there'll be a big reward offered for them – a thousand dollars, sure. That's our money! Now we'll trot in and see the folks. And mind you we don't know anything about any murder, or any di'monds, or any thieves – don't you forget that.'

I had to sigh a little over the way he had got it fixed. I'd a *sold* them di'monds – yes, sir – for twelve thousand dollars; but I didn't say anything. It wouldn't done any good. I says:

'But what are we going to tell your Aunt Sally has made us so long getting down here from the village, Tom?'

'Oh, I'll leave that to you,' he says. 'I reckon you can explain it somehow.'

He was always just that strict and delicate. He never would tell a lie himself.

We struck across the big yard, noticing this, that, and t'other thing that was so familiar, and we so glad to see it again, and when we got to the roofed big passageway betwixt the double log house and the kitchen part, there was everything hanging on the wall just as it used to was, even to Uncle Silas' old faded green baize working-gown with the hood to it, and raggedy white patch between the shoulders that always looked like somebody had hit him with a snowball; and then we lifted the latch and walked in. Aunt Sally she was just a-ripping and a-tearing around, and the children was huddled in one corner, and the old man he was huddled in the other and praying for help in time of need. She jumped for us with joy and tears running down her face and give us a whacking box on the ear, and then hugged us and kissed us and boxed us again, and just couldn't seem to get enough of it, she was so glad to see us; and she says:

'Where *have* you been a-loafing to, you good-for-nothing trash! I've been that worried about you I didn't know what to do. Your traps has been here ever so long, and I've had supper cooked fresh about four times so as to have it hot and good when you come, till at last my patience is just plumb wore out, and I declare I – I – why I could skin you alive! You must be starving, poor things! – set down, set down, everybody; don't lose no more time.'

It was good to be there again behind all that noble corn pone and spareribs, and everything that you could ever want in this world. Old Uncle Silas he peeled off one of his bulliest old-time blessings, with as many layers to it as an onion, and whilst the angels was hauling in the slack of it I was trying to study up what to say about what kept us so long. When our plates was all loadened and we'd got a-going, she asked me, and I says:

'Well, you see – er – Mizzes –'

'Huck Finn! Since when am I Mizzes to you? Have I ever been stingy of cuffs or kisses for you since the day you stood in this room and I took you for Tom Sawyer and blessed God for sending you to me, though you told me four thousand lies and I believed every one of them like a simpleton? Call me Aunt Sally – like you always done.'

So I done it. And I says:

'Well, me and Tom allowed we would come along afoot and take a smell of the woods, and we run across Lem Beebe and Jim Lane, and they asked us to go with them blackberrying tonight, and said they could borrow Jubiter Dunlap's dog, because he had told them just that minute –'

'Where did they see him?' says the old man; and when I looked up to see how *he* come to take an intrust in a little thing like that, his eyes was just burning into me, he was that eager. It surprised me so it kind of throwed me off, but I pulled myself together again and says:

'It was when he was spading up some ground along with you, towards sundown or along there.'

He only said, 'Um,' in a kind of a disappointed way, and didn't take no more intrust. So I went on. I says:

'Well, then, as I was a-saying –'

'That'll do, you needn't go no furder.' It was Aunt Sally. She was boring right into me with her eyes, and very indignant. 'Huck Finn,' she says, 'how'd them men come to talk about going a-blackberrying in September – in *this* region?'

I see I had slipped up, and I couldn't say a word. She waited, still a-gazing at me, then she says:

'And how'd they come to strike that idiot idea of going a-blackberrying in the night?'

'Well, m'm, they – er – they told us they had a lantern, and –'

'Oh, *shet* up – do! Looky here; what was they going to do with a dog? – hunt blackberries with it?'

'I think, m'm, they –'

'Now, Tom Sawyer, what kind of a lie are you fixing *your* mouth to contribit to this mess of rubbage? Speak out – and I warn you before you begin, that I don't believe a word of it. You and Huck's been up to something you no business to – I know it perfectly well; I know you, *both* of you. Now you explain that dog, and them blackberries, and the lantern, and the rest of that rot – and mind you talk as straight as a string – do you hear?'

Tom he looked considerable hurt, and says, very dignified:

'It is a pity if Huck is to be talked to that way, just for making a little bit of a mistake that anybody could make.'

'What mistake has he made?'

'Why, only the mistake of saying blackberries when of course he meant strawberries.'

'Tom Sawyer, I lay if you aggravate me a little more, I'll –'

'Aunt Sally, without knowing it – and of course without intending it – you are in the wrong. If you'd a studied natural history the way you ought, you would know that all over the world except just here in Arkansaw they *always* hunt strawberries with a dog – and a lantern –'

But she busted in on him there and just piled into him and snowed him under. She was so mad she couldn't get the words out fast enough, and she gushed them out in one everlasting freshet. That was what Tom Sawyer was after. He allowed to work her up and get her started and then leave her alone and let her burn herself out. Then she would be so aggravated with that subject that she wouldn't say another word about it, nor let anybody else. Well, it happened just so. When she was tuckered out and had to hold up, he says, quite ca'm:

'And yet, all the same, Aunt Sally –'

'Shet up!' she says, 'I don't want to hear another word out of you.'

So we was perfectly safe, then, and didn't have no more trouble about that delay. Tom done it elegant.

CHAPTER SEVEN

A Night's Vigil

Benny she was looking pretty sober, and she sighed some, now and then; but pretty soon she got to asking about Mary, and Sid, and Tom's Aunt Polly, and then Aunt Sally's clouds cleared off and she got in a good humor and joined in on the questions and was her lovingest best self, and so the rest of the supper went along gay and pleasant. But the old man he didn't take any hand hardly, and was absent-minded and restless, and done a considerable amount of sighing; and it was kind of heartbreaking to see him so sad and troubled and worried.

By and by, a spell after supper, come a nigger and knocked on the door and put his head in with his old straw hat in his hand bowing and scraping, and said his Marse Brace was out at the stile and wanted his brother, and was getting tired waiting supper for him, and would Marse Silas please tell him where he was? I never see Uncle Silas speak up so sharp and fractious before. He says:

'Am I his brother's keeper?'[5]

And then he kind of wilted together, and looked like he wished he hadn't spoken so, and then he says, very gentle: 'But you needn't say that, Billy; I was took sudden and irritable, and I ain't very well these days, and not hardly responsible. Tell him he ain't here.'

And when the nigger was gone he got up and walked the floor, backwards and forwards, mumbling and muttering to himself and plowing his hands through his hair. It was real pitiful to see him. Aunt Sally she whispered to us and told us not to take notice of him, it embarrassed him. She said he was always thinking and thinking, since these troubles come on, and she allowed he didn't more'n about half know what he was about when the thinking spells was on him; and she said he walked in his sleep considerable more now than he used to, and sometimes wandered around over the house and even outdoors in his sleep, and if we catched him at it we must let him alone and not disturb him. She said she reckoned it didn't do him no harm, and maybe it done him good. She said Benny was the only one that was much help to him these days. Said Benny appeared to know just when to try to soothe him and when to leave him alone.

So he kept on tramping up and down the floor and muttering, till by and by he begun to look pretty tired; then Benny she went and snuggled up to his side and put one hand in his and one arm around his waist and walked with him; and he smiled down on her, and reached down and kissed her; and so, little by little the trouble went out of his face and she persuaded him off to his room. They had very petting ways together, and it was uncommon pretty to see.

Aunt Sally she was busy getting the children ready for bed; so by and by it got dull and tedious, and me and Tom took a turn in the moonlight, and fetched up in the watermelon patch and et one, and had a good deal of talk. And Tom said he'd bet the quarreling was all Jubiter's fault, and he was going to be on hand the first time he got a chance, and see; and if it was so, he was going to do his level best to get Uncle Silas to turn him off.

And so we talked and smoked and stuffed watermelon as much as two hours, and then it was pretty late, and when we got back the house was quiet and dark, and everybody gone to bed.

Tom he always seen everything, and now he see that the old

green baize work-gown was gone, and said it wasn't gone when he went out; so he allowed it was curious, and then we went up to bed.

We could hear Benny stirring around in her room, which was next to ourn, and judged she was worried a good deal about her father and couldn't sleep. We found we couldn't, neither. So we set up a long time, and smoked and talked in a low voice, and felt pretty dull and downhearted. We talked the murder and the ghost over and over again, and got so creepy and crawly we couldn't get sleepy nohow and noway.

By and by, when it was away late in the night and all the sounds was late sounds and solemn, Tom nudged me and whispers to me to look, and I done it, and there we see a man poking around in the yard like he didn't know just what he wanted to do, but it was pretty dim and we couldn't see him good. Then he started for the stile, and as he went over it the moon came out strong, and he had a long-handled shovel over his shoulder, and we see the white patch on the old work-gown. So Tom says:

'He's a-walking in his sleep. I wish we was allowed to follow him and see where he's going to. There, he's turned down by the tobacker-field. Out of sight now. It's a dreadful pity he can't rest no better.'

We waited a long time, but he didn't come back any more, or if he did he come around the other way; so at last we was tuckered out and went to sleep and had nightmares, a million of them. But before dawn we was awake again, because meantime a storm had come up and been raging, and the thunder and lightning was awful, and the wind was a-thrashing the trees around, and the rain was driving down in slanting sheets, and the gullies was running rivers. Tom says:

'Looky here, Huck, I'll tell you one thing that's mighty

curious. Up to the time we went out last night the family hadn't heard about Jake Dunlap being murdered. Now the men that chased Hal Clayton and Bud Dixon away would spread the thing around in a half an hour, and every neighbor that heard it would shin out and fly around from one farm to t'other and try to be the first to tell the news. Land, they don't have such a big thing as that to tell twice in thirty year! Huck, it's mighty strange; I don't understand it.'

So then he was in a fidget for the rain to let up, so we could turn out and run across some of the people and see if they would say anything about it to us. And he said if they did we must be horribly surprised and shocked.

We was out and gone the minute the rain stopped. It was just broad day then. We loafed along up the road, and now and then met a person and stopped and said howdy, and told them when we come, and how we left the folks at home, and how long we was going to stay, and all that, but none of them said a word about that thing; which was just astonishing, and no mistake. Tom said he believed if we went to the sycamores we would find that body laying there solitary and alone, and not a soul around. Said he believed the men chased the thieves so far into the woods that the thieves prob'ly seen a good chance and turned on them at last, and maybe they all killed each other, and so there wasn't anybody left to tell.

First we knowed, gabbling along that away, we was right at the sycamores. The cold chills trickled down my back and I wouldn't budge another step, for all Tom's persuading. But he couldn't hold in; he'd *got* to see if the boots was safe on that body yet. So he crope in – and the next minute out he come again with his eyes bulging he was so excited, and says:

'Huck, it's gone!'

I *was* astonished! I says:

'Tom, you don't mean it.'

'It's gone, sure. There ain't a sign of it. The ground is trampled some, but if there was any blood it's all washed away by the storm, for it's all puddles and slush in there.'

At last I give in, and went and took a look myself; and it was just as Tom said – there wasn't a sign of a corpse.

'Dern it,' I says, 'the di'monds is gone. Don't you reckon the thieves slunk back and lugged him off, Tom?'

'Looks like it. It just does. Now where'd they hide him, do you reckon?'

'I don't know,' I says, disgusted, 'and what's more I don't care. They've got the boots, and that's all I cared about. He'll lay around these woods a long time before I hunt him up.'

Tom didn't feel no more intrust in him neither, only curiosity to know what come of him; but he said we'd lay low and keep dark and it wouldn't be long till the dogs or somebody rousted him out.

We went back home to breakfast ever so bothered and put out and disappointed and swindled. I warn't ever so down on a corpse before.

CHAPTER EIGHT

Talking with the Ghost

It warn't very cheerful at breakfast. Aunt Sally she looked old and tired and let the children snarl and fuss at one another and didn't seem to notice it was going on, which wasn't her usual style; me and Tom had a plenty to think about without talking; Benny she looked like she hadn't had much sleep, and whenever she'd lift her head a little and steal a look towards her father you could see there was tears in her eyes; and as for the old man, his things stayed on his plate and got cold without him knowing they was there, I reckon, for he was thinking and thinking all the time, and never said a word and never et a bite.

By and by when it was stillest, that nigger's head was poked in at the door again, and he said his Marse Brace was getting powerful uneasy about Marse Jubiter, which hadn't come home yet, and would Marse Silas please –

He was looking at Uncle Silas, and he stopped there, like the rest of his words was froze; for Uncle Silas he rose up shaky and steadied himself leaning his fingers on the table, and he was panting, and his eyes was set on the nigger, and he kept swallowing, and put his other hand up to his throat a couple of times, and at last he got his words started, and says:

'Does he – does he – think – *what* does he think! Tell him – tell him –' Then he sunk down in his chair limp and weak, and says, so as you could hardly hear him: 'Go away – go away!'

The nigger looked scared and cleared out, and we all felt – well, I don't know how we felt, but it was awful, with the old man panting there, and his eyes set and looking like a person that was dying. None of us could budge; but Benny she slid around soft, with her tears running down, and stood by his side, and nestled his old gray head up against her and begun to stroke it and pet it with her hands, and nodded to us to go away, and we done it, going out very quiet, like the dead was there.

Me and Tom struck out for the woods mighty solemn, and saying how different it was now to what it was last summer when we was here and everything was so peaceful and happy and everybody thought so much of Uncle Silas, and he was so cheerful and simple-hearted and pudd'n-headed and good – and now look at him. If he hadn't lost his mind he wasn't much short of it. That was what we allowed.

It was a most lovely day now, and bright and sunshiny; and the further and further we went over the hills towards the prairie the lovelier and lovelier the trees and flowers got to be and the more it seemed strange and somehow wrong that there had to be trouble in such a world as this. And then all of a sudden I catched my breath and grabbed Tom's arm, and all my livers and lungs and things fell down into my legs.

'There it is!' I says. We jumped back behind a bush shivering, and Tom says:

'Sh! – don't make a noise.'

It was setting on a log right in the edge of a little prairie, thinking. I tried to get Tom to come away, but he wouldn't, and I dasn't budge by myself. He said we mightn't ever get another chance to see one, and he was going to look his fill at this one if he died for it. So I looked too, though it give me the fantods[6] to do it. Tom he *had* to talk, but he talked low.

He says:

'Poor Jakey, it's got all its things on, just as he said he would. *Now* you see what we wasn't certain about – its hair. It's not long now the way it was: it's got it cropped close to its head,

43

the way he said he would. Huck, I never see anything look any more naturaler than what *it* does.'

'Nor I neither,' I says; 'I'd reconnise it anywheres.'

'So would I. It looks perfectly solid and genuwyne, just the way it done before it died.'

So we kept a-gazing. Pretty soon Tom says:

'Huck, there's something mighty curious about this one, don't you know? *It* oughtn't to be going around in the daytime.'

'That's so, Tom – I never heard the like of it before.'

'No, sir, they don't ever come out only at night – and then not till after twelve. There's something wrong about this one, now you mark my words. I don't believe it's got any right to be around in the daytime. But don't it look natural! Jake was going to play deef and dumb here, so the neighbors wouldn't know his voice. Do you reckon it would do that if we was to holler at it?'

'Lordy, Tom, don't talk so! If you was to holler at it I'd die in my tracks.'

'Don't you worry, I ain't going to holler at it. Look, Huck, it's a-scratching its head – don't you see?'

'Well, what of it?'

'Why, this. What's the sense of it scratching its head? There ain't anything there to itch; its head is made out of fog or something like that, and can't itch. A fog can't itch; any fool knows that.'

'Well, then, if it don't itch and can't itch, what in the nation is it scratching it for? Ain't it just habit, don't you reckon?'

'No, sir, I don't. I ain't a bit satisfied about the way this one acts. I've a blame good notion it's a bogus one – I have, as sure as I'm a-sitting here. Because, if it – Huck!'

'Well, what's the matter now?'

'*You can't see the bushes through it!*'

'Why, Tom, it's so, sure! It's as solid as a cow. I sort of begin to think –'

'Huck, it's biting off a chaw of tobacker! By George, *they* don't chaw – they hain't got anything to chaw *with*. Huck!'

'I'm a-listening.'

'It ain't a ghost at all. It's Jake Dunlap his own self!'

'Oh, your granny!' I says.

'Huck Finn, did we find any corpse in the sycamores?'

'No.'

'Or any sign of one?'

'No.'

'Mighty good reason. Hadn't ever been any corpse there.'

'Why, Tom, you know we heard –'

'Yes, we did – heard a howl or two. Does that prove anybody was killed? Course it don't. And we seen four men run, then this one come walking out and we took it for a ghost. No more ghost than you are. It was Jake Dunlap his own self, and it's Jake Dunlap now. He's been and got his hair cropped, the way he said he would, and he's playing himself for a stranger, just the same as he said he would. Ghost? Hum! – he's as sound as a nut.'

Then I see it all, and how we had took too much for granted. I was powerful glad he didn't get killed, and so was Tom, and we wondered which he would like the best – for us to never let on to know him, or how? Tom reckoned the best way would be to go and ask him. So he started; but I kept a little behind, because I didn't know but it might be a ghost, after all. When Tom got to where he was, he says:

'Me and Huck's mighty glad to see you again, and you needn't be afeared we'll tell. And if you think it'll be safer for you if we don't let on to know you when we run across you, say the word and you'll see you can depend on us, and would ruther cut our hands off than get you into the least little bit of danger.'

First off he looked surprised to see us, and not very glad, either; but as Tom went on he looked pleasanter, and when he was done he smiled, and nodded his head several times, and made signs with his hands, and says:

'Goo-goo – goo-goo,' the way deef and dummies does. Just then we see some of Steve Nickerson's people coming that lived t'other side of the prairie, so Tom says:

'You do it elegant; I never see anybody do it better. You're right; play it on us, too; play it on us same as the others; it'll keep you in practice and prevent you making blunders. We'll keep away from you and let on we don't know you, but any time we can be any help, you just let us know.'

Then we loafed along past the Nickersons, and of course they asked if that was the new stranger yonder, and where'd he come from, and what was his name, and which communion was he, Babtis' or Methodis', and which politics, Whig or Democrat, and how long is he staying, and all them other questions that humans always asks when a stranger comes, and animals does, too. But Tom said he warn't able to make anything out of deef and dumb signs, and the same with goo-gooing. Then we watched them go and bullyrag Jake; because we was pretty uneasy for him. Tom said it would take him days to get so he wouldn't forget he was a deef and dummy sometimes, and speak out before he thought. When we had watched long enough to see that Jake was getting along all right and working his signs very good, we loafed along again, allowing to strike the schoolhouse about recess time, which was a three-mile tramp.

I was so disappointed not to hear Jake tell about the row in the sycamores, and how near he come to getting killed, that I couldn't seem to get over it, and Tom he felt the same, but said if we was in Jake's fix we would want to go careful and keep still and not take any chances.

The boys and girls was all glad to see us again, and we had a real good time all through recess. Coming to school the Henderson boys had come across the new deef and dummy and told the rest; so all the scholars was chuck full of him and couldn't talk about anything else, and was in a sweat to get a sight of him because they hadn't ever seen a deef and dummy in their lives, and it made a powerful excitement.

Tom said it was tough to have to keep mum now; said we would be heroes if we could come out and tell all we knowed; but after all, it was still more heroic to keep mum, there warn't two boys in a million could do it. That was Tom Sawyer's idea about it, and reckoned there warn't anybody could better it.

CHAPTER NINE

Finding of Jubiter Dunlap

In the next two or three days Dummy he got to be powerful popular. He went associating around with the neighbors, and they made much of him, and was proud to have such a rattling curiosity among them. They had him to breakfast, they had him to dinner, they had him to supper; they kept him loaded up with hog and hominy[7], and warn't ever tired staring at him and wondering over him, and wishing they knowed more about him, he was so uncommon and romantic. His signs warn't no good; people couldn't understand them and he prob'ly couldn't himself, but he done a sight of goo-gooing, and so everybody was satisfied, and admired to hear him go it. He toted a piece of slate around, and a pencil; and people wrote questions on it and he wrote answers; but there warn't anybody could read his writing but Brace Dunlap. Brace said he couldn't read it very good, but he could manage to dig out the meaning most of the time. He said Dummy said he belonged away off somers and used to be well off, but got busted by swindlers which he had trusted, and was poor now, and hadn't any way to make a living.

Everybody praised Brace Dunlap for being so good to that stranger. He let him have a little log cabin all to himself, and had his niggers take care of it, and fetch him all the vittles he wanted.

Dummy was at our house some, because old Uncle Silas was so afflicted himself, these days, that anybody else that was afflicted was a comfort to him. Me and Tom didn't let on that we had knowed him before, and he didn't let on that he had knowed us before. The family talked their troubles out before him the same as if he wasn't there, but we reckoned it wasn't any harm for him to hear what they said. Gener'ly he didn't seem to notice, but sometimes he did.

Well, two or three days went along, and everybody got to getting uneasy about Jubiter Dunlap. Everybody was asking everybody if they had any idea what had become of him. No, they hadn't, they said: and they shook their heads and said there was something powerful strange about it. Another and another day went by; then there was a report got around that praps he was murdered. You bet it made a big stir! Everybody's tongue was clacking away after that. Saturday two or three gangs turned out and hunted the woods to see if they could run across his remainders. Me and Tom helped, and it was noble good times and exciting. Tom he was so brimful of it he couldn't eat nor rest. He said if we could find that corpse we would be celebrated, and more talked about than if we got drownded.

The others got tired and give it up; but not Tom Sawyer – that warn't his style. Saturday night he didn't sleep any, hardly, trying to think up a plan; and towards daylight in the morning he struck it. He snaked me out of bed and was all excited, and says:

'Quick, Huck, snatch on your clothes – I've got it! Bloodhound!'

In two minutes we was tearing up the river road in the dark towards the village. Old Jeff Hooker had a bloodhound, and Tom was going to borrow him. I says:

'The trail's too old, Tom – and besides, it's rained, you know.'

'It don't make any difference, Huck. If the body's hid in the woods anywhere around the hound will find it. If he's been

49

murdered and buried, they wouldn't bury him deep, it ain't likely, and if the dog goes over the spot he'll scent him, sure. Huck, we're going to be celebrated, sure as you're born!'

He was just a-blazing; and whenever he got afire he was most likely to get afire all over. That was the way this time. In two minutes he had got it all ciphered out, and wasn't only just going to find the corpse – no, he was going to get on the track of that murderer and hunt *him* down, too; and not only that, but he was going to stick to him till –

'Well,' I says, 'you better find the corpse first; I reckon that's a-plenty for today. For all we know, there *ain't* any corpse and nobody hain't been murdered. That cuss could a gone off somers and not been killed at all.'

That gravelled him, and he says:

'Huck Finn, I never see such a person as you to want to spoil everything. As long as *you* can't see anything hopeful in a thing, you won't let anybody else. What good can it do you to throw cold water on that corpse and get up that selfish theory that there ain't been any murder? None in the world. I don't see how you can act so. I wouldn't treat you like that, and you know it. Here we've got a noble good opportunity to make a ruputation, and –'

'Oh, go ahead,' I says. 'I'm sorry, and I take it all back. I didn't mean nothing. Fix it any way you want it. *He* ain't any consequence to me. If he's killed, I'm as glad of it as you are; and if he –'

'I never said anything about being glad; I only –'

'Well, then, I'm as *sorry* as you are. Any way you druther have it, that is the way I druther have it. He –'

'There ain't any druthers *about* it, Huck Finn; nobody said anything about druthers. And as for –'

He forgot he was talking, and went tramping along,

studying. He begun to get excited again, and pretty soon he says:

'Huck, it'll be the bulliest thing that ever happened if we find the body after everybody else has quit looking, and then go ahead and hunt up the murderer. It won't only be an honor to us, but it'll be an honor to Uncle Silas because it was us that done it. It'll set him up again, you see if it don't.'

But Old Jeff Hooker he throwed cold water on the whole business when we got to his blacksmith shop and told him what we come for.

'You can take the dog,' he says, 'but you ain't a-going to find any corpse, because there ain't any corpse to find. Everybody's quit looking, and they're right. Soon as they come to think, they knowed there warn't no corpse. And I'll tell you for why. What does a person kill another person for, Tom Sawyer? – answer me that.'

'Why, he – er –'

'Answer up! You ain't no fool. What does he kill him *for*?'

'Well, sometimes it's for revenge, and –'

'Wait. One thing at a time. Revenge, says you; and right you are. Now who ever had anything agin that poor trifling no-account? Who do you reckon would want to kill *him*? – that rabbit!'

Tom was stuck. I reckon he hadn't thought of a person having to have a *reason* for killing a person before, and now he sees it warn't likely anybody would have that much of a grudge against a lamb like Jubiter Dunlap. The blacksmith says, by and by:

'The revenge idea won't work, you see. Well, then, what's next? Robbery? B'gosh, that must a been it, Tom! Yes, sirree, I reckon we've struck it this time. Some feller wanted his gallus-buckles, and so he –'

But it was so funny he busted out laughing, and just went on laughing and laughing and laughing till he was 'most dead, and Tom looked so put out and cheap that I knowed he was ashamed he had come, and he wished he hadn't. But old Hooker never let up on him. He raked up everything a person ever could want to kill another person about, and any fool could see they didn't any of them fit this case, and he just made no end of fun of the whole business and of the people that had been hunting the body; and he said –

'If they'd had any sense they'd a knowed the lazy cuss slid out because he wanted a loafing spell after all this work. He'll come pottering back in a couple of weeks, and then how'll you fellers feel? But, laws bless you, take the dog, and go and hunt his remainders. Do, Tom.'

Then he busted out, and had another of them forty-rod laughs of his'n. Tom couldn't back down after all this, so he said, 'All right, unchain him!' and the blacksmith done it, and we started home and left that old man laughing yet.

It was a lovely dog. There ain't any dog that's got a lovelier disposition than a bloodhound, and this one knowed us and liked us. He capered and raced around ever so friendly, and powerful glad to be free and have a holiday; but Tom was so cut up he couldn't take any intrust in him, and said he wished he'd stopped and thought a minute before he ever started on such a fool errand. He said old Jeff Hooker would tell everybody, and we'd never hear the last of it.

So we loafed along home down the back lanes, feeling pretty glum and not talking. When we was passing the far corner of our tobacker-field we heard the dog set up a long howl in there, and we went to the place and he was scratching the ground with all his might, and every now and then canting up his head sideways and fetching another howl.

It was a long square, the shape of a grave; the rain had made it sink down and show the shape. The minute we come and stood there we looked at one another and never said a word. When the dog had dug down only a few inches he grabbed something and pulled it up, and it was an arm and a sleeve. Tom kind of gasped out, and says:

'Come away, Huck – it's found.'

I just felt awful. We struck for the road and fetched the first men that come along. They got a spade at the crib and dug out the body, and you never see such an excitement. You couldn't make anything out of the face, but you didn't need to. Everybody said:

'Poor Jubiter; it's his clothes, to the last rag!'

Some rushed off to spread the news and tell the justice of the peace and have an inquest, and me and Tom lit out for the house. Tom was all afire and 'most out of breath when we come tearing in where Uncle Silas and Aunt Sally and Benny was. Tom sung out:

'Me and Huck's found Jubiter Dunlap's corpse all by ourselves with a bloodhound, after everybody else had quit hunting and given it up; and if it hadn't a been for us it never *would* a been found; and he *was* murdered too – they done it with a club or something like that; and I'm going to start in and find the murderer, next, and I bet I'll do it!'

Aunt Sally and Benny sprung up pale and astonished, but Uncle Silas fell right forward out of his chair onto the floor and groans out:

'Oh, my God, you've found him *now*!'

CHAPTER TEN

The Arrest of Uncle Silas

Them awful words froze us solid. We couldn't move hand or foot for as much as half a minute. Then we kind of come to, and lifted the old man up and got him into his chair, and Benny petted him and kissed him and tried to comfort him, and poor old Aunt Sally she done the same; but, poor things, they was so broke up and scared and knocked out of their right minds that they didn't hardly know what they was about. With Tom it was awful; it 'most petrified him to think maybe he had got his uncle into a thousand times more trouble than ever, and maybe it wouldn't ever happened if he hadn't been so ambitious to get celebrated, and let the corpse alone the way the others done. But pretty soon he sort of come to himself again and says:

'Uncle Silas, don't you say another word like that. It's dangerous, and there ain't a shadder of truth in it.'

Aunt Sally and Benny was thankful to hear him say that, and they said the same; but the old man he wagged his head sorrowful and hopeless, and the tears run down his face, and he says:

'No – I done it; poor Jubiter, I done it!'

It was dreadful to hear him say it. Then he went on and told about it, and said it happened the day me and Tom come – along about sundown. He said Jubiter pestered him and aggravated him till he was so mad he just sort of lost his mind and grabbed up a stick and hit him over the head with all his might, and Jubiter dropped in his tracks. Then he was scared and sorry, and got down on his knees and lifted his head up, and begged him to speak and say he wasn't dead; and before long he come to, and when he see who it was holding his head, he jumped like he was 'most scared to death, and cleared the fence and tore into the woods, and was gone. So he hoped he wasn't hurt bad.

'But laws,' he says, 'it was only just fear that gave him that last little spurt of strength, and of course it soon played out and he laid down in the bush, and there wasn't anybody to help him, and he died.'

Then the old man cried and grieved, and said he was a murderer and the mark of Cain was on him, and he had disgraced his family and was going to be found out and hung. But Tom said:

'No, you ain't going to be found out. You *didn't* kill him. *One* lick wouldn't kill him. Somebody else done it.'

'Oh, yes,' he says, 'I done it – nobody else. Who else had anything against him? Who else *could* have anything against him?'

He looked up kind of like he hoped some of us could mention somebody that could have a grudge against that harmless no-account, but of course it warn't no use – he *had* us; we couldn't say a word. He noticed that, and he saddened down again, and I never see a face so miserable and so pitiful to see. Tom had a sudden idea, and says:

'But hold on! – somebody *buried* him. Now who –'

He shut off sudden. I knowed the reason. It give me the cold shudders when he said them words, because right away I remembered about us seeing Uncle Silas prowling around with a long-handled shovel away in the night that night. And I knowed Benny seen him, too, because she was talking about it one day. The minute Tom shut off he changed the subject and went to begging Uncle Silas to keep mum, and the rest of us done the same, and said he *must*, and said it wasn't his business to tell on himself, and if he kept mum nobody would ever know; but if it was found out and any harm come to him it would break the family's hearts and kill them, and yet never do anybody any good. So at last he promised. We was all of us more comfortable, then, and went to work to cheer up the old man. We told him all he'd got to do was to keep still, and it wouldn't be long till the whole thing would blow over and be forgot. We all said there wouldn't anybody ever suspect Uncle Silas, nor ever dream of such a thing, he being so good and kind, and having such a good character; and Tom says, cordial and hearty, he says –

'Why, just look at it a minute; just consider. Here is Uncle Silas, all these years a preacher – at his own expense; all these years doing good with all his might and every way he can think of – at his own expense, all the time; always been loved by everybody, and respected; always been peaceable and minding his own business, the very last man in this whole deestrict to touch a person, and everybody knows it. Suspect *him*? Why, it ain't any more possible than –'

'By authority of the State of Arkansaw, I arrest you for the murder of Jubiter Dunlap!' shouts the sheriff at the door.

It was awful. Aunt Sally and Benny flung themselves at Uncle Silas, screaming and crying, and hugged him and hung to him, and Aunt Sally said go away, she wouldn't ever give him up, they shouldn't have him, and the niggers they come crowding and crying to the door and – well, I couldn't stand it; it was enough to break a person's heart; so I got out.

They took him up to the little one-horse jail in the village, and we all went along to tell him goodbye; and Tom was feeling elegant, and says to me, 'We'll have a most noble good time and heaps of danger some dark night getting him out of there, Huck, and it'll be talked about everywheres and we will be celebrated.' But the old man busted that scheme up the minute he whispered to him about it. He said no, it was his duty to stand whatever the law done to him, and he would stick to the jail plumb through to the end, even if there warn't no door to it. It disappointed Tom and gravelled him a good deal, but he had to put up with it.

But he felt responsible and bound to get his Uncle Silas free; and he told Aunt Sally, the last thing, not to worry, because he was going to turn in and work night and day and beat this game and fetch Uncle Silas out innocent; and she was very loving to him and thanked him and said she knowed he would do his very best. And she told us to help Benny take care of the house and the children, and then we had a goodbye cry all around and went back to the farm, and left her there to live with the jailer's wife a month till the trial in October.

CHAPTER ELEVEN

Tom Sawyer Discovers the Murderers

Well, that was a hard month on us all. Poor Benny, she kept up the best she could, and me and Tom tried to keep things cheerful there at the house, but it kind of went for nothing, as you may say. It was the same up at the jail. We went up every day to see the old people, but it was awful dreary, because the old man warn't sleeping much, and was walking in his sleep considerable and so he got to looking fagged and miserable, and his mind got shaky, and we all got afraid his troubles would break him down and kill him. And whenever we tried to persuade him to feel cheerfuler, he only shook his head and said if we only knowed what it was to carry around a murderer's load in your heart we wouldn't talk that way. Tom and all of us kept telling him it *wasn't* murder, but just accidental killing, but it never made any difference – it was murder, and he wouldn't have it any other way. He actu'ly begun to come out plain and square towards trial time and acknowledge that he *tried* to kill the man. Why, that was awful, you know. It made things seem fifty times as dreadful, and there warn't no more comfort for Aunt Sally and Benny. But he promised he wouldn't say a word about his murder when others was around, and we was glad of that.

Tom Sawyer racked the head off of himself all that month trying to plan some way out for Uncle Silas, and many's the night he kept me up 'most all night with this kind of tiresome work, but he couldn't seem to get on the right track no way. As for me, I reckoned a body might as well give it up, it all looked so blue and I was so downhearted; but he wouldn't. He stuck to the business right along, and went on planning and thinking and ransacking his head.

So at last the trial come on, towards the middle of October, and we was all in the court. The place was jammed, of course. Poor old Uncle Silas, he looked more like a dead person than a live one, his eyes was so hollow and he looked so thin and so mournful. Benny she set on one side of him and Aunt Sally on the other, and they had veils on, and was full of trouble. But Tom he set by our lawyer, and had his finger in everwheres, of course. The lawyer let him, and the judge let him. He 'most took the business out of the lawyer's hands sometimes; which was well enough, because that was only a mud-turtle of a back-settlement lawyer and didn't know enough to come in when it rains, as the saying is.

They swore in the jury, and then the lawyer for the prostitution got up and begun. He made a terrible speech against the old man, that made him moan and groan, and made Benny and Aunt Sally cry. The way *he* told about the murder kind of knocked us all stupid, it was so different from the old man's tale. He said he was going to prove that Uncle Silas was *seen* to kill Jubiter Dunlap by two good witnesses, and done it deliberate, and *said* he was going to kill him the very minute he hit him with the club; and they seen him hide Jubiter in the bushes, and they seen that Jubiter was stone dead. And said Uncle Silas come later and lugged Jubiter down into the tobacker-field, and two men seen him do it. And said Uncle Silas turned out, away in the night, and buried Jubiter, and a man seen him at it.

I says to myself, poor old Uncle Silas has been lying about it because he reckoned nobody seen him and he couldn't bear to break Aunt Sally's heart and Benny's; and right he was: as for me, I would a lied the same way, and so would anybody that had any feeling, to save them such misery and sorrow which *they* warn't no ways responsible for. Well, it made our lawyer look pretty sick; and it knocked Tom silly, too, for a little spell, but then he braced up and let on that he warn't worried – but I knowed he *was*, all the same. And the people – my, but it made a stir amongst them!

And when that lawyer was done telling the jury what he was going to prove, he set down and begun to work his witnesses.

First, he called a lot of them to show that there was bad blood betwixt Uncle Silas and the diseased; and they told how they had heard Uncle Silas threaten the diseased, at one time and another, and how it got worse and worse and everybody was talking about it, and how diseased got afraid of his life, and told two or three of them he was certain Uncle Silas would up and kill him some time or another.

Tom and our lawyer asked them some questions; but it warn't no use, they stuck to what they said.

Next, they called up Lem Beebe, and he took the stand. It come into my mind, then, how Lem and Jim Lane had come along talking, that time, about borrowing a dog or something from Jubiter Dunlap; and that brought up the blackberries and the lantern; and that brought up Bill and Jack Withers, and how they passed by, talking about a nigger stealing Uncle Silas' corn; and that fetched up our old ghost that come along about the same time and scared us so – and here *he* was too, and a privileged character, on accounts of his being deef and dumb and a stranger, and they had fixed him a chair inside the railing, where he could cross his legs and be comfortable, whilst the other people was all in a jam so they couldn't hardly breathe. So it all come back to me just the way it was that day; and it made me mournful to think how pleasant it was up to then, and how miserable ever since.

Lem Beebe, sworn, said – 'I was a-coming along, that day, 2nd of September, and Jim Lane was with me, and it was towards sundown, and we heard loud talk, like quarreling, and we was very close, only the hazel bushes between (that's along the fence); and we heard a voice say, "I've told you more'n once I'd kill you," and knowed it was this prisoner's voice; and then we see a club come up above the bushes and down out of sight again, and heard a smashing thump and then a groan or two: and then we crope soft to where we could see, and there laid Jupiter Dunlap dead, and this prisoner standing over him with the club; and the next he hauled the dead man into a clump of bushes and hid him, and then we stooped low, to be cut of sight, and got away.'

Well, it was awful. It kind of froze everybody's blood to hear it, and the house was 'most as still whilst he was telling it as if there warn't nobody in it. And when he was done, you could hear them gasp and sigh, all over the house, and look at one another the same as to say, 'Ain't it perfectly terrible – ain't it awful!' Now happened a thing that astonished me. All the time the first witnesses was proving the bad blood and the threats and all that, Tom Sawyer was alive and laying for them; and the minute they was through, he went for them, and done his level best to catch them in lies and spile their testimony. But now, how different. When Lem first begun to talk, and never said anything about speaking to Jubiter or trying to borrow a dog off of him, he was all alive and laying for Lem, and you could see he was getting ready to cross-question him to death pretty soon, and then I judged him and me would go on the stand by and by and tell what we heard him and Jim Lane say. But the next time I looked at Tom I got the cold shivers. Why, he was in the brownest study you ever see – miles and miles away. He warn't hearing a word Lem Beebe was saying; and when he got through he was still in that brown study, just the same. Our lawyer joggled him, and then he looked up startled, and says, 'Take the witness if you want him. Lemme alone – I want to think.'

Well, that beat me. I couldn't understand it. And Benny and her mother – oh, they looked sick, they was so troubled. They shoved their veils to one side and tried to get his eye, but it warn't any use, and I couldn't get his eye either. So the mud-turtle he tackled the witness, but it didn't amount to nothing; and he made a mess of it.

Then they called up Jim Lane, and he told the very same story over again, exact. Tom never listened to this one at all, but set there thinking and thinking, miles and miles away. So the mud-turtle went in alone again and come out just as flat as he done before. The lawyer for the prostitution looked very comfortable, but the judge looked disgusted. You see, Tom was just the same as a regular lawyer, nearly, because it was Arkansaw law for a prisoner to choose anybody he wanted to help his lawyer, and Tom had had Uncle Silas shove him into the case, and now he was botching it and you could see the judge didn't like it much. All that the mud-turtle got out of Lem and Jim was this: he asked them:

'Why didn't you go and tell what you saw?'

'We was afraid we would get mixed up in it ourselves. And we was just starting down the river a-hunting for all the week besides; but as soon as we come back we found out they'd been searching for the body, so then we went and told Brace Dunlap all about it.'

'When was that?'

'Saturday night, September 9th.'

The judge he spoke up and says: 'Mr Sheriff, arrest these

two witnesses on suspicions of being accessionary after the fact to the murder.'

The lawyer for the prostitution jumps up all excited, and says: 'Your honor! I protest against this extraordi –'

'Set down!' says the judge, pulling his bowie and laying it on his pulpit.

'I beg you to respect the court.'

So he done it. Then he called Bill Withers.

Bill Withers, sworn, said: 'I was coming along about sundown, Saturday, September 2nd, by the prisoner's field, and my brother Jack was with me and we seen a man toting off something heavy on his back and allowed it was a nigger stealing corn; we couldn't see distinct; next we made out that it was one man carrying another; and the way it hung, so kind of limp, we judged it was somebody that was drunk; and by the man's walk we said it was Parson Silas, and we judged he had found Sam Cooper drunk in the road, which he was always trying to reform him, and was toting him out of danger.'

It made the people shiver to think of poor old Uncle Silas toting off the diseased down to the place in his tobacker-field where the dog dug up the body, but there warn't much sympathy around amongst the faces, and I heard one cuss say, 'It's the coldest blooded work I ever struck, lugging a murdered man around like that, and going to bury him like a animal, and him a preacher at that.'

Tom he went on thinking, and never took no notice; so our lawyer took the witness and done the best he could, and it was plenty poor enough.

Then Jack Withers he come on the stand and told the same tale, just like Bill done.

And after him comes Brace Dunlap, and he was looking very mournful, and 'most crying; and there was a rustle and a stir all around, and everybody got ready to listen, and lots of the women folks said, 'Poor cretur, poor cretur,' and you could see a many of them wiping their eyes.

Brace Dunlap, sworn, said: 'I was in considerable trouble a long time about my poor brother, but I reckoned things warn't near so bad as he made out, and I couldn't make myself believe anybody would have the heart to hurt a poor harmless cretur like that' – (by jings, I was sure I seen Tom give a kind of a faint little start, and then look disappointed again) – 'and you know I *couldn't* think a preacher would hurt him – it warn't natural to think such an onlikely thing – so I never paid much attention, and now I sha'n't ever, ever forgive myself; for if I had a done different, my poor brother would be with me this day, and not laying yonder murdered, and him so harmless.' He kind of broke down there and choked up, and waited to get his voice; and people all around said the most pitiful things, and women cried; and it was very still in there, and solemn, and old Uncle Silas, poor thing, he give a groan right out so everybody heard him. Then Brace he went on, 'Saturday, September 2nd, he didn't come home to supper. By and by I got a little uneasy, and one of my niggers went over to this prisoner's place, but come back and said he warn't there. So I got uneasier and uneasier, and couldn't rest. I went to bed, but I couldn't sleep; and turned out, away late in the night, and went wandering over to this prisoner's place and all around about there a good while, hoping I would run across my poor brother, and never knowing he was out of his troubles and gone to a better shore –' So he broke down and choked up again, and 'most all the women was crying now. Pretty soon he got another start and says: 'But it warn't no use; so at last I went home and tried to get some sleep, but couldn't. Well, in a day or two everybody was uneasy, and they got to talking

64

about this prisoner's threats, and took to the idea, which I didn't take no stock in, that my brother was murdered so they hunted around and tried to find his body, but couldn't and give it up. And so I reckoned he was gone off somers to have a little peace, and would come back to us when his troubles was kind of healed. But late Saturday night, the 9th, Lem Beebe and Jim Lane come to my house and told me all – told me the whole awful 'sassination, and my heart was broke. And *then* I remembered something that hadn't took no hold of me at the time, because reports said this prisoner had took to walking in his sleep and doing all kind of things of no consequence, not knowing what he was about. I will tell you what that thing was that come back into my memory. Away late that awful Saturday night when I was wandering around about this prisoner's place, grieving and troubled, I was down by the corner of the tobacker-field and I heard a sound like digging in a gritty soil; and I crope nearer and peeped through the vines that hung on the rail fence and seen this prisoner *shoveling* – shoveling with a long-handled shovel – heaving earth into a big hole that was 'most filled up; his back was to me, but it was bright moonlight and I knowed him by his old green baize work-gown with a splattery white patch in the middle of the back like somebody had hit him with a snowball. *He was burying the man he'd murdered!'*

And he slumped down in his chair crying and sobbing, and 'most everybody in the house busted out wailing, and crying, and saying, 'Oh, it's awful – awful – horrible! and there was a most tremendous excitement, and you couldn't hear yourself think; and right in the midst of it up jumps old Uncle Silas, white as a sheet, and sings out:

'*It's true, every word – I murdered him in cold blood!*'

By Jackson, it petrified them! People rose up wild all over

the house, straining and staring for a better look at him, and the judge was hammering with his mallet and the sheriff yelling, 'Order – order in the court – order!'

And all the while the old man stood there a-quaking and his eyes a-burning, and not looking at his wife and daughter, which was clinging to him and begging him to keep still, but pawing them off with his hands and saying he *would* clear his black soul from crime, he *would* heave off this load that was more than he could bear, and he *wouldn't* bear it another hour! And then he raged right along with his awful tale, everybody a-staring and gasping, judge, jury, lawyers, and everybody, and Benny and Aunt Sally crying their hearts out. And by George, Tom Sawyer never looked at him once! Never once – just set there gazing with all his eyes at something else, I couldn't tell what. And so the old man raged right along, pouring his words out like a stream of fire:

'I killed him! I am guilty! But I never had the notion in my life to hurt him or harm him, spite of all them lies about my threatening him, till the very minute I raised the club – then my heart went cold! – then the pity all went out of it, and I struck to kill! In that one moment all my wrongs come into my mind; all the insults that that man and the scoundrel his brother, there, had put upon me, and how they laid in together to ruin me with the people, and take away my good name, and *drive* me to some deed that would destroy me and my family that hadn't ever done *them* no harm, so help me God! And they done it in a mean revenge – for why? Because my innocent pure girl here at my side wouldn't marry that rich, insolent, ignorant coward, Brace Dunlap, who's been sniveling here over a brother he never cared a brass farthing for –' (I see Tom give a jump and look glad *this* time, to a dead certainty) '– and in that moment I've told you about, I forgot

66

my God and remembered only my heart's bitterness – God forgive me – and I struck to kill. In one second I was miserably sorry – oh, filled with remorse; but I thought of my poor family, and I *must* hide what I'd done for their sakes; and I did hide that corpse in the bushes; and presently I carried it to the tobacker-field; and in the deep night I went with my shovel and buried it where –'

Up jumps Tom and shouts:

'*Now*, I've got it!' and waves his hand, oh, ever so fine and starchy, towards the old man, and says:

'Set down! A murder *was* done, but you never had no hand in it!'

Well, sir, you could a heard a pin drop. And the old man he sunk down kind of bewildered in his seat and Aunt Sally and Benny didn't know it, because they was so astonished and staring at Tom with their mouths open and not knowing what they was about. And the whole house the same. I never seen people look so helpless and tangled up, and I hain't ever seen eyes bug out and gaze without a blink the way theirn did. Tom says, perfectly ca'm:

'Your honor, may I speak?'

'For God's sake, yes – go on!' says the judge, so astonished and mixed up he didn't know what he was about hardly.

Then Tom he stood there and waited a second or two – that was for to work up an 'effect', as he calls it – then he started in just as ca'm as ever, and says:

'For about two weeks now there's been a little bill sticking on the front of this courthouse offering two thousand dollars reward for a couple of big di'monds – stole at St Louis. Them di'monds is worth twelve thousand dollars. But never mind about that till I get to it. Now about this murder. I will tell you all about it – how it happened – who done it – every detail.'

You could see everybody nestle now, and begin to listen for all they was worth.

'This man here, Brace Dunlap, that's been sniveling so about his dead brother that *you* know he never cared a straw for, wanted to marry that young girl there, and she wouldn't have him. So he told Uncle Silas he would make him sorry. Uncle Silas knowed how powerful he was, and how little chance he had against such a man, and he was scared and worried, and done everything he could think of to smooth him over and get him to be good to him: he even took his no-account brother Jubiter on the farm and give him wages and stinted his own family to pay them; and Jubiter done everything his brother could contrive to insult Uncle Silas, and fret and worry him, and try to drive Uncle Silas into doing him a hurt, so as to injure Uncle Silas with the people. And it done it. Everybody turned against him and said the meanest kind of things about him, and it graduly broke his heart – yes, and he was so worried and distressed that often he warn't hardly in his right mind.

'Well, on that Saturday that we've had so much trouble about, two of these witnesses here, Lem Beebe and Jim Lane, come along by where Uncle Silas and Jubiter Dunlap was at work – and that much of what they've said is true, the rest is lies. They didn't hear Uncle Silas say he would kill Jubiter; they didn't hear no blow struck; they didn't see no dead man, and they didn't see Uncle Silas hide anything in the bushes. Look at them now – how they set there, wishing they hadn't been so handy with their tongues; anyway, they'll wish it before I get done.

'That same Saturday evening Bill and Jack Withers *did* see one man lugging off another one. That much of what they said is true, and the rest is lies. First off they thought it was a nigger

68

stealing Uncle Silas' corn – you notice it makes them look silly, now, to find out somebody overheard them say that. That's because they found out by and by who it was that was doing the lugging, and *they* know best why they swore here that they took it for Uncle Silas by the gait – which it *wasn't*, and they knowed it when they swore to that lie.

'A man out in the moonlight *did* see a murdered person put underground in the tobacker-field – but it wasn't Uncle Silas that done the burying. He was in his bed at that very time.

'Now, then, before I go on, I want to ask you if you've ever noticed this: that people, when they're thinking deep, or when they're worried, are 'most always doing something with their hands, and they don't know it, and don't notice what it is their hands are doing. Some stroke their chins; some stroke their noses; some stroke up *under* their chin with their hand; some twirl a chain, some fumble a button, then there's some that draws a figure or a letter with their finger on their cheek, or under their chin or on their under lip. That's *my* way. When I'm restless, or worried, or thinking hard, I draw capital V's on my cheek or on my under lip or under my chin, and never anything *but* capital V's – and half the time I don't notice it and don't know I'm doing it.'

That was odd. That is just what I do; only I make an O. And I could see people nodding to one another, same as they do when they mean '*that*'s so'.

'Now, then, I'll go on. That same Saturday – no, it was the night before – there was a steamboat laying at Flagler's Landing, forty miles above here, and it was raining and storming like the nation. And there was a thief aboard, and he had them two big di'monds that's advertised out here on this courthouse door; and he slipped ashore with his handbag and struck out into the dark and the storm, and he was a-hoping he could get to this town all right and be safe. But he had two pals aboard the boat, hiding, and he knowed they was going to kill him the first chance they got and take the di'monds; because all three stole them, and then this fellow he got hold of them and skipped.

'Well, he hadn't been gone more'n ten minutes before his pals found it out, and they jumped ashore and lit out after him. Prob'ly they burnt matches and found his tracks. Anyway, they dogged along after him all day Saturday and kept out of his sight; and towards sundown he come to the bunch of sycamores down by Uncle Silas' field, and he went in there to get a disguise out of his handbag and put it on before he showed himself here in the town – and mind you he done that just a little after the time that Uncle Silas was hitting Jubiter Dunlap over the head with a club – for he *did* hit him.

'But the minute the pals see that thief slide into the bunch of sycamores, they jumped out of the bushes and slid in after him.

'They fell on him and clubbed him to death.

'Yes, for all he screamed and howled so, they never had no mercy on him, but clubbed him to death. And two men that was running along the road heard him yelling that way, and they made a rush into the sycamore bunch – which was where they was bound for, anyway – and when the pals saw them they lit out and the two new men after them a-chasing them as tight as they could go. But only a minute or two – then these two new men slipped back very quiet into the sycamores.

'*Then* what did they do? I will tell you what they done. They found where the thief had got his disguise out of his carpet-sack to put on; so one of them strips and puts on that disguise.'

Tom waited a little here, for some more 'effect' – then he says, very deliberate:

'The man that put on that dead man's disguise was – *Jubiter Dunlap!*'

'Great Scott!' everybody shouted, all over the house, and old Uncle Silas he looked perfectly astonished.

'Yes, it was Jubiter Dunlap. Not dead, you see. Then they pulled off the dead man's boots and put Jubiter Dunlap's old ragged shoes on the corpse and put the corpse's boots on Jubiter Dunlap. Then Jubiter Dunlap stayed where he was, and the other man lugged the dead body off in the twilight; and after midnight he went to Uncle Silas' house, and took his old green work-robe off of the peg where it always hangs in the passage betwixt the house and the kitchen and put it on, and stole the long-handled shovel and went off down into the tobacker-field and buried the murdered man.'

He stopped, and stood half a minute. Then –

'And who do you reckon the murdered man *was?* It was – *Jake* Dunlap, the long-lost burglar!'

'Great Scott!'

'And the man that buried him was – *Brace* Dunlap, his brother!'

'Great Scott!'

'And who do you reckon is this mowing idiot here that's letting on all these weeks to be a deef and dumb stranger? It's – *Jubiter* Dunlap!'

My land, they all busted out in a howl, and you never see the like of that excitement since the day you was born. And Tom he made a jump for Jubiter and snaked off his goggles and his false whiskers, and there was the murdered man, sure enough, just as alive as anybody! And Aunt Sally and Benny they went to hugging and crying and kissing and smothering old Uncle Silas to that degree he was more muddled and confused and mushed up in his mind than he ever was before, and that is saying considerable. And next, people begun to yell:

'Tom Sawyer! Tom Sawyer! Shut up everybody, and let him go on! Go on, Tom Sawyer!'

Which made him feel uncommon bully, for it was nuts for Tom Sawyer to be a public character thataway, and a hero, as he calls it. So when it was all quiet, he says:

'There ain't much left, only this. When that man there, Brace Dunlap, had 'most worried the life and sense out of Uncle Silas till at last he plumb lost his mind and hit this other blatherskite, his brother, with a club, I reckon he seen his chance. Jubiter broke for the woods to hide, and I reckon the game was for him to slide out, in the night, and leave the country. Then Brace would make everybody believe Uncle Silas killed him and hid his body somers; and that would ruin Uncle Silas and drive *him* out of the country – hang him, maybe; I dunno. But when they found their dead brother in the sycamores without knowing him, because he was so battered up, they see they had a better thing; disguise *both* and bury Jake and dig him up presently all dressed up in Jubiter's clothes, and hire Jim Lane and Bill Withers and the others to swear to some handy lies – which they done. And there they set, now, and I told them they would be looking sick before I got done, and that is the way they're looking now.

'Well, me and Huck Finn here, we come down on the boat with the thieves, and the dead one told us all about the di'monds, and said the others would murder him if they got the chance; and we was going to help him all we could. We was bound for the sycamores when we heard them killing him in there; but we was in there in the early morning after the storm and allowed nobody hadn't been killed, after all. And when we see Jubiter Dunlap here spreading around in the very same disguise Jake told us *he* was going to wear, we thought it was Jake his own self – and he was goo-gooing deef and dumb, and *that* was according to agreement.

'Well, me and Huck went on hunting for the corpse after the others quit, and we found it. And was proud, too; but Uncle Silas he knocked us crazy by telling us *he* killed the man. So we was mighty sorry we found the body, and was bound to save Uncle Silas' neck if we could; and it was going to be tough work, too, because he wouldn't let us break him out of prison the way we done with our old nigger Jim, you remember.

'I done everything I could the whole month to think up some way to save Uncle Silas, but I couldn't strike a thing. So when we come into court today I come empty, and couldn't see no chance anywheres. But by and by I had a glimpse of something that set me thinking – just a little wee glimpse – only that, and not enough to make sure; but it set me thinking hard – and *watching*, when I was only letting on to think; and by and by, sure enough, when Uncle Silas was piling out that stuff about *him* killing Jubiter Dunlap, I catched that glimpse again, and this time I jumped up and shut down the proceedings, because I *knowed* Jubiter Dunlap was a-setting here before me. I knowed him by a thing which I seen him do – and I remembered it. I'd seen him do it when I was here a year ago.'

He stopped then, and studied a minute – laying for an 'effect' – I knowed it perfectly well. Then he turned off like he was going to leave the platform, and says, kind of lazy and indifferent:

'Well, I believe that is all.'

Why, you never heard such a howl! – and it come from the whole house:

'What *was* it you seen him do? Stay where you are, you little devil! You think you are going to work a body up till his mouth's a-watering and stop there? What *was* it he done?'

That was it, you see – he just done it to get an 'effect'; you couldn't a pulled him off of that platform with a yoke of oxen.

'Oh, it wasn't anything much,' he says. 'I seen him looking a little excited when he found Uncle Silas was actuly fixing to hang himself for a murder that warn't ever done; and he got more and more nervous and worried, I a-watching him sharp but not seeming to look at him – and all of a sudden his hands begun to work and fidget, and pretty soon his left crept up and *his finger drawed a cross on his cheek, and then I had him!*'

Well, then they ripped and howled and stomped and clapped their hands till Tom Sawyer was that proud and happy he didn't know what to do with himself. And then the judge he looked down over his pulpit and says:

'My boy, did you *see* all the various details of this strange conspiracy and tragedy that you've been describing?'

'No, your honor, I didn't see any of them.'

'Didn't see any of them! Why, you've told the whole history straight through, just the same as if you'd seen it with your eyes. How did you manage that?'

Tom says, kind of easy and comfortable –

'Oh, just noticing the evidence and piecing this and that together, your honor; just an ordinary little bit of detective work; anybody could a done it.'

'Nothing of the kind! Not two in a million could a done it. You are a very remarkable boy.'

Then they let go and give Tom another smashing round, and he – well, he wouldn't a sold out for a silver mine. Then the judge says:

'But are you certain you've got this curious history straight?'

'Perfectly, your honor. Here is Brace Dunlap – let him deny his share of it if he wants to take the chance; I'll engage to make him wish he hadn't said anything... Well, you see *he's* pretty quiet. And his brother's pretty quiet, and them four witnesses that lied so and got paid for it, they're pretty quiet. And as for Uncle Silas, it ain't any use for him to put in his oar, I wouldn't believe him under oath!'

Well, sir, that fairly made them shout; and even the judge he let go and laughed. Tom he was just feeling like a rainbow. When they was done laughing he looks up at the judge and says:

'Your honor, there's a thief in this house.'

'A thief?'

'Yes, sir. And he's got them twelve-thousand-dollar di'monds on him.'

By gracious, but it made a stir! Everybody went shouting:

'Which is him? which is him? p'int him out!'

And the judge says:

'Point him out, my lad. Sheriff, you will arrest him. Which one is it?'

Tom says: 'This late dead man here – Jubiter Dunlap.'

Then there was another thundering let-go of astonishment and excitement; but Jubiter, which was astonished enough before, was just fairly putrified with astonishment this time. And he spoke up, about half crying, and says:

'Now *that's* a lie. Your honor, it ain't fair; I'm plenty bad enough without that. I done the other things – Brace he put me up to it, and persuaded me, and promised he'd make me rich, some day, and I done it, and I'm sorry I done it, and I wisht I hadn't; but I hain't stole no di'monds, and I hain't *got* no di'monds; I wisht I may never stir if it ain't so. The sheriff can search me and see.'

Tom says:

'Your honor, it wasn't right to call him a thief, and I'll let up on that a little. He did steal the di'monds, but he didn't know it. He stole them from his brother Jake when he was laying dead, after Jake had stole them from the other thieves; but Jubiter didn't know he was stealing them; and he's been swelling around here with them a month; yes, sir, twelve thousand dollars' worth of di'monds on him – all that riches, and going around here every day just like a poor man. Yes, your honor, he's got them on him now.'

The judge spoke up and says:

'Search him, sheriff.'

Well, sir, the sheriff he ransacked him high and low, and everywhere: searched his hat, socks, seams, boots, everything – and Tom he stood there quiet, laying for another of them effects of his'n. Finally the sheriff he give it up, and everybody looked disappointed, and Jubiter says:

'There, now! what'd I tell you?'

And the judge says: 'It appears you were mistaken this time, my boy.'

Then Tom took an attitude and let on to be studying with all his might, and scratching his head. Then all of a sudden he glanced up chipper, and says:

'Oh, now I've got it ! I'd forgot.'

Which was a lie, and I knowed it. Then he says: 'Will somebody be good enough to lend me a little small screw-driver? There was one in your brother's handbag that you smouched, Jubiter, but I reckon you didn't fetch it with you.'

'No, I didn't. I didn't want it, and I give it away.'

'That's because you didn't know what it was for.'

Jubiter had his boots on again, by now, and when the thing Tom wanted was passed over the people's heads till it got to him, he says to Jubiter:

'Put up your foot on this chair.' And he kneeled down and begun to unscrew the heel-plate, everybody watching; and when he got that big di'mond out of that boot-heel and held it up and let it flash and blaze and squirt sunlight everwhich-away, it just took everybody's breath; and Jubiter he looked so sick and sorry you never see the like of it. And when Tom held up the other di'mond he looked sorrier than ever. Land! he was thinking how he would a skipped out and been rich and independent in a foreign land if he'd only had the luck to guess what the screwdriver was in the carpet-bag for. Well, it was a most exciting time, take it all around, and Tom got cords of glory. The judge took the di'monds, and stood up in his pulpit, and cleared his throat, and shoved his spectacles back on his head, and says:

'I'll keep them and notify the owners; and when they send for them it will be a real pleasure to me to hand you the two thousand dollars, for you've earned the money – yes, and you've earned the deepest and most sincerest thanks of this community besides, for lifting a wronged and innocent family out of ruin and shame, and saving a good and honorable man from a felon's death, and for exposing to infamy and the punishment of the law a cruel and odious scoundrel and his miserable creatures!'

Well, sir, if there'd been a brass band to bust out some music, then, it would a been just the perfectest thing I ever see, and Tom Sawyer he said the same.

Then the sheriff he nabbed Brace Dunlap and his crowd, and by and by next month the judge had them up for trial and jailed the whole lot. And everybody crowded back to Uncle

Silas' little old church, and was ever so loving and kind to him and the family and couldn't do enough for them; and Uncle Silas he preached them the blamedest jumbledest idiotic sermons you ever struck, and would tangle you up so you couldn't find your way home in daylight; but the people never let on but what they thought it was the clearest and brightest and elegantest sermons that ever was; and they would set there and cry, for love and pity; but, by George, they give me the jim-jams and the fantods and caked up what brains I had, and turned them solid; but by and by they loved the old man's intellects back into him again, and he was as sound in his skull as ever he was, which ain't no flattery, I reckon. And so the whole family was as happy as birds, and nobody could be gratefuller and lovinger than what they was to Tom Sawyer; and the same to me, though I hadn't done nothing. And when the two thousand dollars come, Tom give half of it to me, and never told anybody so, which didn't surprise me, because I knowed him.

AUTHOR'S NOTE

Strange as the incidents of this story are, they are not inventions, but facts – even to the public confession of the accused. I take them from an old-time Swedish criminal trial, change the actors, and transfer the scenes to America. I have added some details, but only a couple of them are important ones.

– Mark Twain

NOTES

1. A reference to an event in Mark Twain's novel, *The Adventures of Huckleberry Finn* (1884).
2. A game played by flipping a pocket knife into the ground.
3. Point-blank.
4. A marshy offshoot of a lake or river, especially in the southern states of America.
5. A reference to Cain's reply to the Lord on being asked where his brother Abel was; Cain had previously attacked his brother in a field and killed him. (Genesis 4:8-10)
6. A state of uneasiness or apprehension, 'the creeps'.
7. A meal of pork and coarsely ground Indian corn.

BIOGRAPHICAL NOTE

Mark Twain was born Samuel Langhorne Clemens in 1835 in Florida. Soon after his birth his family moved to Hannibal, Missouri, where he spent his childhood. Following his father's death in 1847, Twain worked as a printer for a newspaper owned by his brother, before finding employment in New York and Philadelphia, again as a printer. From 1857 to 1861, he worked as a river pilot on the Mississippi, before moving firstly to Virginia City, and then to California to take up a position as a newspaper correspondent. A successful short story in 1865 quickly inspired a collection entitled *The Celebrated Jumping Frog of Calaveras County, and Other Sketches* (1867), and further volumes swiftly followed. With striking effect, Twain prioritised the method of telling a story over its outcome, and, though a prolific writer of satires, travelogues, essays, and letters, he is best remembered for his picaresque depictions of Missouri life: namely his 1876 novel, *The Adventures of Tom Sawyer*, and its sequel, *The Adventures of Huckleberry Finn* (1884).

In 1870 Twain married Olivia Langdon. Her death in 1904, together with the loss of their daughter, Susy, and the onset of financial difficulties in the 1890s, had an impact on Twain's later work; potboilers were written for money, and other works became darker in tone. Twain spent much of the 1890s in Europe, residing by turns in England, Switzerland, Austria and France, before returning to New York in 1900 and then settling in Connecticut. He died on the 21st April 1910.

HESPERUS PRESS CLASSICS

Hesperus Press, as suggested by the Latin motto, is
committed to bringing near what is far – far both in space
and time. Works written by the greatest authors, and unjustly
neglected or simply little known in the English-speaking
world, are made accessible through new translations and a
completely fresh editorial approach. Through these classic
works, the reader is introduced to the greatest writers from
all times and all cultures.

For more information on Hesperus Press, please visit our
website: **www.hesperuspress.com**

ET REMOTISSIMA PROPE

SELECTED TITLES FROM HESPERUS PRESS

Author	Title	Foreword writer
Louisa May Alcott	*Behind a Mask*	Doris Lessing
Pedro Antonio de Alarcon	*The Three-Cornered Hat*	
Pietro Aretino	*The School of Whoredom*	Paul Bailey
Jane Austen	*Love and Friendship*	Fay Weldon
Honoré de Balzac	*Colonel Chabert*	A.N. Wilson
Charles Baudelaire	*On Wine and Hashish*	Margaret Drabble
Aphra Behn	*The Lover's Watch*	
Giovanni Boccaccio	*Life of Dante*	A.N. Wilson
Charlotte Brontë	*The Green Dwarf*	Libby Purves
Mikhail Bulgakov	*The Fatal Eggs*	Doris Lessing
Giacomo Casanova	*The Duel*	Tim Parks
Miguel de Cervantes	*The Dialogue of the Dogs*	
Anton Chekhov	*The Story of a Nobody*	Louis de Bernières
Anton Chekhov	*Three Years*	William Fiennes
Wilkie Collins	*Who Killed Zebedee?*	Martin Jarvis
Arthur Conan Doyle	*The Tragedy of the Korosko*	Tony Robinson
William Congreve	*Incognita*	Peter Ackroyd
Joseph Conrad	*Heart of Darkness*	A.N. Wilson
Joseph Conrad	*The Return*	Colm Tóibín
Gabriele D'Annunzio	*The Book of the Virgins*	Tim Parks
Dante Alighieri	*New Life*	Louis de Bernières
Daniel Defoe	*The King of Pirates*	Peter Ackroyd
Marquis de Sade	*Incest*	Janet Street-Porter
Charles Dickens	*The Haunted House*	Peter Ackroyd
Charles Dickens	*A House to Let*	
Fyodor Dostoevsky	*The Double*	Jeremy Dyson
Fyodor Dostoevsky	*Poor People*	Charlotte Hobson
Joseph von Eichendorff	*Life of a Good-for-nothing*	
George Eliot	*Amos Barton*	Matthew Sweet

Henry Fielding	*Jonathan Wild the Great*	Peter Ackroyd
F. Scott Fitzgerald	*The Rich Boy*	John Updike
Gustave Flaubert	*Memoirs of a Madman*	Germaine Greer
E.M. Forster	*Arctic Summer*	Anita Desai
Ugo Foscolo	*Last Letters of Jacopo Ortis*	Valerio Massimo Manfredi
Giuseppe Garibaldi	*My Life*	Tim Parks
Elizabeth Gaskell	*Lois the Witch*	Jenny Uglow
Théophile Gautier	*The Jinx*	Gilbert Adair
André Gide	*Theseus*	
Nikolai Gogol	*The Squabble*	Patrick McCabe
Thomas Hardy	*Fellow-Townsmen*	Emma Tennant
L.P. Hartley	*Simonetta Perkins*	Margaret Drabble
Nathaniel Hawthorne	*Rappaccini's Daughter*	Simon Schama
E.T.A. Hoffmann	*Mademoiselle de Scudéri*	Gilbert Adair
Victor Hugo	*The Last Day of a Condemned Man*	Libby Purves
Joris-Karl Huysmans	*With the Flow*	Simon Callow
Henry James	*In the Cage*	Libby Purves
Franz Kafka	*Metamorphosis*	Martin Jarvis
John Keats	*Fugitive Poems*	Andrew Motion
Heinrich von Kleist	*The Marquise of O–*	Andrew Miller
D.H. Lawrence	*Daughters of the Vicar*	Anita Desai
D.H. Lawrence	*The Fox*	Doris Lessing
Leonardo da Vinci	*Prophecies*	Eraldo Affinati
Giacomo Leopardi	*Thoughts*	Edoardo Albinati
Nikolai Leskov	*Lady Macbeth of Mtsensk*	Gilbert Adair
Niccolò Machiavelli	*Life of Castruccio Castracani*	Richard Overy
Katherine Mansfield	*In a German Pension*	Linda Grant
Guy de Maupassant	*Butterball*	Germaine Greer
Lorenzino de' Medici	*Apology for a Murder*	Tim Parks
Herman Melville	*The Enchanted Isles*	Margaret Drabble

Prosper Mérimée	*Carmen*	Philip Pullman
Sándor Petőfi	*John the Valiant*	George Szirtes
Francis Petrarch	*My Secret Book*	Germaine Greer
Luigi Pirandello	*Loveless Love*	
Edgar Allan Poe	*Eureka*	Sir Patrick Moore
Alexander Pope	*The Rape of the Lock and A Key to the Lock*	Peter Ackroyd
Alexander Pope	*Scriblerus*	Peter Ackroyd
Antoine François Prévost	*Manon Lescaut*	Germaine Greer
Marcel Proust	*Pleasures and Days*	A.N. Wilson
Alexander Pushkin	*Dubrovsky*	Patrick Neate
François Rabelais	*Gargantua*	Paul Bailey
François Rabelais	*Pantagruel*	Paul Bailey
Friedrich von Schiller	*The Ghost-seer*	Martin Jarvis
Percy Bysshe Shelley	*Zastrozzi*	Germaine Greer
Stendhal	*Memoirs of an Egotist*	Doris Lessing
Robert Louis Stevenson	*Dr Jekyll and Mr Hyde*	Helen Dunmore
Theodor Storm	*The Lake of the Bees*	Alan Sillitoe
Italo Svevo	*A Perfect Hoax*	Tim Parks
Jonathan Swift	*Directions to Servants*	Colm Tóibín
W.M. Thackeray	*Rebecca and Rowena*	Matthew Sweet
Leo Tolstoy	*Hadji Murat*	Colm Tóibín
Ivan Turgenev	*Faust*	Simon Callow
Mark Twain	*The Diary of Adam and Eve*	John Updike
Giovanni Verga	*Life in the Country*	Paul Bailey
Jules Verne	*A Fantasy of Dr Ox*	Gilbert Adair
Edith Wharton	*The Touchstone*	Salley Vickers
Oscar Wilde	*The Portrait of Mr W.H.*	Peter Ackroyd
Virginia Woolf	*Carlyle's House and Other Sketches*	Doris Lessing
Virginia Woolf	*Monday or Tuesday*	Scarlett Thomas
Emile Zola	*For a Night of Love*	A.N. Wilson